THE ESCAPE Artist

MAYRA ARAUJO

PAGE PUBLISHING, INC.
New York, NY

First originally published by Page Publishing, Inc. 2019

ISBN 978-1-64462-704-4 (Paperback)
ISBN 978-1-64462-706-8 (Digital)

Printed in the United States of America

This book is dedicated to my favorite Uncle, Antonio Moran, who always wanted to become an author, but couldn't for circumstances out of his control. You were my inspiration to write, and you will always be an author to me.

To my mom, son and daughter, thanks for your support and encouragement.

Thanks to all my family and friends for believing in me.

Chapter 1

I t was a cold, rainy day in October. There was a
different feel in the air. It seems that the scorch-
ing hot temperature from the previous weeks was
gone for now. The leaves were beginning to turn different colors, a welcome change after what seemed
to be an endless summer. One could see different
hues of red, orange, and yellow on the trees in the
backyard.

This past summer had been long and hot, and
everyone welcomed the changed in temperature.

Anna looked out through her room's foggy window. It had been raining all morning, and the sky was
a sad and melancholic shade of gray, but Anna did
not mind the rain. She had been looking forward to
today all week. She had barely been able to sleep at all
last night just thinking about it.

Today was the first time that Anna had been
absent from school this year. She usually didn't miss
school. She was in the third grade now, and they
had been planning the Halloween dance at school.
Normally, she wouldn't want to miss class. She loved
her teacher Mrs. McCarthey, and her best friend
Makayla and her were in the same class this year.

She always looked forward to attending school, but today was the only day her mom was off from work this week, and she had promised Anna to take her.

She had asked her mom for a cat for a very long time, and today they were going to the Humane Society to find one.

As they got in the car, Anna could hardly contain her excitement. She had been wanting a pet all her life. It had been very hard to convince her mom to get one. Her mom worked very long hours at the diner and hardly had time for her brother and her, let alone a pet.

Dogs were too much work, too needy, her mom had argued, and too loud for the small house they lived in. Besides, who was going to train it and walk it on winter days?

Cats, on the other hand, were very independent. They didn't mind being left alone for long periods of time, and they clean themselves. So after long talks and consideration, they had decided on a cat.

Anna never had a pet before, but she always envied people that owned one. It would be nice to have something to cuddle with and keep her company when her mom was working. She hated being alone, and being with her brother Kevin was just as bad as being alone. He was six years older than she was, and he had his own friends. He didn't want to bother with her. So now her cat would keep her company. Besides, it was going to be nice to have a pet to love and care for. Life was going to be so much better as a cat owner, she thought. She couldn't believe it was actually happening. She wanted a pet for so long, and today was the day. Today she was getting her own cat.

"Anna, are you sure you would be able to take care of this cat on your own? I want to make sure we are in the same page about this before we make any decision. Owning a cat is a big responsibility, and I don't want to be the one who ends up taking care of it."

"I know, Mom. You already told me. You won't even know it's there, I promise."

Anna looked out the car window. The rain was hitting the windowpanes, making all the streets, houses, and trees look bleary and distorted. She couldn't see where they were, but the Humane Society was close to her house, only a few miles away. She was sure they were close to it. The car made a sharp left into the shopping mall; they were finally there.

"Hi, good morning," said the lady behind the counter. "Is there anything I can help you with?"

"Yes, we are thinking about adopting a cat for my daughter."

"Oh, sure, that would be great. We currently have more cats than we can handle right now, and even with all the volunteers and foster homes, it's still very hard to keep up, being October and all. It would really be nice if we could find one of these cats a good home."

"Yes, that's the idea," replied Mrs. Wellington. "But if you don't mind me asking, why is October any different than any other month when it comes to adopting a cat?"

"Well, we usually have a higher volume of cats this month, especially black cats, since it's illegal to sell or adopt black cats until after Halloween."

"Wow, I didn't know that."

"Yes, most people don't know, but I guess they worry about people using cats as sacrifices in ritual ceremonies and that sort of things on Halloween night. One never knows this days. So we have about ten black cats now that we don't know what to do with. A lot of extra work. Also, people don't stop bringing cats in. Even when the store is close. Just last week, we found yet another black cat in a crate that someone dropped off in front of the store overnight. Like I said, it never ends."

"Mom, can we see it please? I can wait to see the kitten."

"Oh, honey, this is not a kitten. I'm afraid he is a little bit older," said the clerk. She was a middle-age woman of about forty-five, a little overweight, plain looking, and she talked too loud. "I will show you to the kitten. We have a few here. I'm sure there'll be one for you. Besides, I'm hoping that cat's still in its cage and not wandering around the store. We have been having a hard time keeping him in his cage." She laughed. "It has gotten out of the cage so many times that the workers named him Houdini. We don't know how he does it, but he manages to get out every night. A real scape artist, I tell you!"

"Oh, Mom, can I see him please? He sounds so much fun! Pleaseeee," Anna whined.

"All the cats are this way," said the clerk. They walked down a long hall with cages on both sides; there were cats of all shapes and colors. Some looked on as they walked by, some were sleeping, oblivious to their presence, and some meowed as they saw them go by, trying to grab their attention. Anna kept looking at the cats as she walked, then they finally stopped.

"Here it is! The kitty section," said the clerk. "Let me know if there is any you would like to see, and I will open the cage door for you."

There were so many cute little kittens. She finally spotted one that she really liked. It was orange and white with blue eyes.

"Mom, I really like this one. Isn't this one cute?"

"Yes, I guess…," she said, not too convinced. "I will go get the clerk."

"No, Mom, stay here. I'll go!" She hurried up to get the clerk, too excited to even think. Then something or someone grabbed her leg from under one of the cages. Anna jumped back and let out a scream.

"Anna, are you okay? What happened, honey?"

"I don't know, Mom. Something grabbed my leg," said Anna, out of breath and pale as a piece of paper.

Anna's mom bent over to see what was underneath the cages. It was pretty dark under there, but she could make out a black silhouette and two almost fluorescent-green eyes that glowed in the dark.

"Oh, Anna honey! I think it's a kitten or a cat, I'm not sure. Nothing to worry about, silly. You almost gave me a heart attack."

"Is everything okay? I heard a scream," said the clerk, rushing down the hall to meet them.

"Oh, nothing really. We are fine now. But I think we just met the cat you were talking about earlier. I think he is down under the cages. He just scared my daughter half to death."

"Yeah! I think you met him, all right. He must be out of his cage again. Let me see," said the clerk, bending down with a lot of difficulty. "Hey, kitty-kitty… Hey, kitty-kitty." She was sticking her hand under the cage and pulling him out.

"Oh, Mom! He is so cute! Can we have this one? Can we take this one home?"

"I don't know about that, Anna. Look at him. He is not even a kitten and—"

"Oh, I'm sorry, but I don't think that's going to be possible anyway," said the clerk. "We have no paperwork done on him yet. We just gave him the shots, but he is not ready to be adopted. Besides, I wouldn't be able to let you adopt him anyway. Like I said earlier, we have a store policy about black cats this time of year."

"But, Mom, look!" said Anna while she held the cat by her two front paws so the cat's chest would be exposed. "He is not completely black. He has a white spot on his chest."

They both turned around to see the cat.

The cat was a young cat, not really a kitten, but not a grown cat either. He had big green eyes. His hair was short and shiny, almost too black. And yes, Anna was right. There was an inverted triangle spot of white hair on the cat's chest.

"I'm afraid I won't be able to let you take this one. I'm sorry. Company policy is company policy. I don't make the rules," said the lady while trying to get the cat back from Anna. The cat was clinging from Anna's shirt and meowing real loud.

"See, Mom? He wants to go home with us. I think he likes me. Mom, pleasee…"

"Are you sure there is nothing you can do?" said Mrs. Wellington. "You have too many cats as it is. You said it yourself. You will be doing both of us a favor if you let us take him home, really! And he is not technically black, anyway. I'm sure they would understand."

"I guess it would be all right," said the clerk, lost in thoughts. The cat had been nothing but trouble since day one. He refused to eat cat food, he was constantly escaping and hiding, and some of the volunteers said they were creeped out by him. They claimed the cat seemed to understand what they were saying, that sometimes he seemed to be listening to their conversations. A little too smart for a cat, they said. Most of them high school kids with a very active imagination, she knew that. It was all nonsense, so silly, but what if he didn't get adopted later? People usually wanted kitties anyway. What would they do with him then? she thought to herself. "Oh, okay. Why not? He is yours if you want him."

As they left the store carrying the cat, Anna was elated. It had taken a while to get all the paperwork done, pay the for the adoption, etc. Almost all morning was gone by now. Soon all her friends would be out of school. She couldn't wait to tell her best friend Makayla about her new cat.

"Mom, what do you think we should call him?"

"I don't know, sweetie. It's your cat. You should be the one to name him, not I."

"A name… a name… How about Toby? That's a cute boy name, right, Mom?"

"Sure! Toby sounds good, but what was the name she said they called him?"

"The name on the paperwork you mean? I think is was Adam," said Anna, looking throughout the papers on her lap. "Yeah, Adam, that's what it says here, but I don't like that name for him."

"No, not that one. I'm talking about the one they gave him at the shelter from escaping so much. Remember? The lady mentioned it?"

"Oh yes! Houdini! Like the escape artist!" Anna was very familiar with that name. Her brother Kevin had gone through a phase where he was really into magic. That was all he talked about. He drove them crazy with all the new tricks he learned. He always tried them on them first. He had even asked for a Criss Angel magic book that Christmas.

"Yes, I like that name. Houdini it is then. Right? Houdini?" she said, petting the cat through the door of the cage. "You're my Houdini, aren't you? Aren't you?"

On the way home, they did a quick stop at a pet store to get cat food. It had stop raining by now. But the day was still gloomy and foggy. There weren't many people at the store being that it was a weekday. They walked up and down the aisles. The amount of cat food choices was really overwhelming. In the cat section, there was every brand of cat food claiming to be better than the other.

"Anna, didn't the lady at the shelter said that he was a really finicky eater, remember? He only ate tuna, I think. Tell you what. Why don't we stop at the supermarket on the way home and get him some tuna and sardines instead. I would hate to waste money on cat food that he is not going to eat."

As they got back to the car, they noticed that the cage was empty.

"Look! Mom, he is out of the cage again and looking out the window." She laughed. The cat perked up his ear, but it seemed to be staring at something far away in the distance.

"Well, you can't say they did not warn us about that. Just put him back in the crate. I don't want to get into a car accident with him lose in the car."

"I know. Come here, Houdini." She grabbed the cat and put him back in the crate. "You are going to get us in trouble. Besides, we are almost home. It won't be long now. No more cages for you. You are going to love it there."

Chapter 2

Anna woke up to a beautiful, crisp, and sunny autumn morning. The sun was out, the birds were chirping, and the sky was blue. It was hard to believe just yesterday it had been raining almost all day.

The first thing on Anna's mind was Houdini. *Was it a dream? Where is he?* she thought, looking around her room. When she spotted him sitting on the windowsill, she breathed a sigh of relief. "Oh, there you are! Got me scared," she said while she petted him. Just then she remembered last night. She had spent almost half the night awake. The cat had been really active last night. She knew that cats were nocturnal, but she wasn't prepared for this.

"Anna, are you coming down for breakfast? Please let your brother know breakfast is ready!" yelled Anna's mom from the bottom of the stairs.

"Good morning, Mom," said Kevin from behind her. "What's all the screaming for?"

"Oh my gosh, Kevin! You scared me. I thought you were sleeping."

"Not really… Actually, I had a very hard time sleeping last night. The stupid cat kept running around the room, trying to open the door, I guess. I could hear him scratching from my room. The noise kept me up, so I went to the basement to play Xbox. And as I passed Anna's room, I saw him sticking his paws under the door, trying to open it. What's the deal with that cat anyway?"

"I don't know, Kevin. I didn't hear anything. Besides, Anna is really happy that she finally got the cat, so please don't start complaining so soon. Let her have her moment please. Let's just have a nice breakfast, okay? I have to be heading out to work soon. Where is your sister?"

"Coming!" said Anna, entering the kitchen.

"Good morning, honey. Take a seat, we are having waffles. Would you like some eggs?"

"Yes, Mom, thanks. Scrambled please."

"How did you sleep last night? Your brother said he heard noises from your room."

"Oh yeah. Houdini slept on my bed last night, but he wouldn't stay still. He kept walking on me, jumping on the windowsill to look outside, turning on the lights… Ugh! I even had to go fetch him from the family room. I don't even know how he got out. I was glad the light was on though. He was sitting on the sofa in front of the TV like he was ready to watch TV. It was so funny!" She laughed.

"Well, you better keep him quiet tonight, or I will tell Mom to take him back. I wanted a dog, remember? Cats are dumb anyway. I don't know why we even got one."

"Kev, stop bothering your sister. Are you ready yet? If you want me to drop you off at soccer practice, we better go now. I don't want to be late for work. Hurry up."

*****

Anna was alone in the house; her mom was working all day, and Kevin was going to a friend's house after practice. She was so glad to have Houdini to keep her company. The house they lived in was really secluded. There were a lot of trees around, and the nearest house was about two blocks away. They lived in a rural area. They only had one neighbor, Mrs. Anderson, the old lady who owned the property and lived in the main house next to them. She lived alone. Her husband had passed away, and they did not have any children. She was the owner of the house they lived in. Their house used to be the guest house.

Anna still wasn't used to living in a place like this, so lonely and desolate. They had moved there right after her mom and dad separated about a year ago. This house was the only place her mom could afford on her own. Anna still missed the friends she had grown up with, her school and her old house, and of course her dad. They only saw their dad one weekend out of the month now. She had always been a daddy's girl, and she missed him a lot. They talked on the phone often, but it wasn't the same as having him in the same house. Things were really different now, she thought as she sat down to watch TV. Houdini lay on the sofa next to her.

Anna surfed through the channels until she found something to watch, a rerun episode of *Drake and Josh*. She was just getting into the show when Houdini jumped on the remote control sitting on the coffee table and changed the channel to CNN news. Something about global warming came on.

"Come here, you," said Anna, retrieving the cat back to her lap and pressing the return key on the remote control. *Drake and Josh* was back on for not even five minutes when Houdini jumped on the remote and changed the channel again. A football game came on. This time Anna grabbed him and tickled him. "You don't like the show, huh, Houdini? You don't like the show?"

The cat freed himself from her and sat back up. And as she stroked his back, she didn't know if it was her imagination. But she could've sworn that she saw the cat smile.

Chapter 3

Time rushed by. It was now the end of October. Almost all the leaves on the trees had changed color, and the temperature was getting lower every day. It had also been raining a lot lately—typical weather for this time of year. Winter would be here soon. Halloween was only two days away. She was going to be a witch this year, and she was taking Houdini as the witch's black cat. She had even purchased a witch's pot to take Houdini inside of it. He was the perfect complement to her costume. Houdini had turned out to be a very special cat. She had heard about cats being mysterious, but he was just too much. He still didn't eat anything but tuna and sardines. Kevin had given him yoo-hoo as a joke once, and now that was all he wanted to drink. He even demanded it by standing in front of the refrigerator, meowing until someone would get it for him. He also would open doors, turn on light switches, flush the toilet, and almost every night go out of the room to watch TV downstairs in the family room. He had scared the bejesus out of them the first time they found him watching television. But by now they were used to it. They all thought it was funny, including Kevin, who was beginning to take a liking to the cat. Now, he thought the cat was cool, not so lame anymore. Now when they heard the TV on at night, they all knew it was the cat, no reason to be alarmed.

Halloween was finally here. All the waiting and the preparation was over. The house was decorated for the festivities, the candy was bought, and they were ready to go. Halloween was going to be great this year. Since the houses around her house were so far apart for a kid to walk from house to house and trick-or-treat, the town had organized a Halloween festival down Main Street. It was called Spooky Fest. People, mostly parents, lined the sidewalk with Halloween-decorated tables and chairs where they sat to give away candy and to enjoy seeing all the little ones dressed in their Halloween costumes. All the children and teenagers dressed up in costumes. There were superheroes, ghost ballerinas, witches, firefighters, and angels.

A lot of the neighbors decorated their tractors and trailers with orange and purple lights, jack-o'-lanterns, and hay, and they made homemade Halloween floats that paraded up and down the street, carrying adults and children and stopping every so often for kids to get down, get candy, and go back up again. Almost all houses on Main Street were decorated for Halloween with pumpkins, orange lights, and inflatable ghosts, witches, monsters, and giant spiders. Scary Halloween music played from different houses. A lot of houses had graveyards on their front lawn with hands sticking out of the ground.

Today was a particularly dark night; the moon wasn't out, so many of the children carried plastic pumpkins with a light inside or flashlights so they could see the way. Being a rural area, the street did not have a lot of streetlights. After sunset it was mostly dark. The lights in their plastic pumpkins with their orange glow resembled floating candles, making the night spookier. There was a chill in the air. It was very windy, and the wind was making a lot of the leaves fall from the trees. The ground was covered with leaves. Some swirled in the air and collected between the street and the sidewalk, and at times it almost looked as if it was raining leaves.

Mom drove Anna and Kevin to the festival around 7:00 p.m. They had been waiting for it to be dark. Kevin was dressed as a prisoner. He had drawn a dollar symbol with a black Sharpie on a white pillowcase to use as a candy bag. A lot of kids were prisoners this year, including some of Kevin's friends.

They walked up and down the street, going in and out of houses, collecting candy. After visiting a few of the houses, they stopped at a house that was heavily decorated for Halloween. The owners of the house had gone to great lengths this Halloween to make this house look like a haunted house. There was a fog machine making everything foggy and scary. Police crime scene tape covered the entrance. Anna had been carrying Houdini inside a plastic candy container that looked like a witch's pot. They were sharing Kevin's pillowcase to carry the candies. They were going to split it once they got home.

Once they got to the front porch of the house, the front door screeched and opened by itself. They heard screams and noises coming from the inside of the house. It was so foggy inside that it was really hard to see. Houdini seemed to be scared this time. He kept trying to get out of the bag, and he was meowing loudly. They kept walking in slowly toward the inside of the house; they knew it was a fake haunted house and it wasn't real, but that did not stop them from being scared. It looked just too real. Houdini never looked so scared. He was clawing Anna's clothes and shaking. As they got to the inside of the house, they saw what looked like a crazy asylum or a mad scientist lab. There were cages lining one of the walls. Inside the cages were fake monkeys, a dog, and even a human reaching his hand out of the cage as if asking for help. Skeletons and bloody human body parts lined the floor.

Houdini was very scared. Anna kept petting him to keep him calm, but she could feel his heart beat against her hand, his heart rate getting faster and stronger. In the middle of the room was a hospital bed like the one in the operating room, and on top of it lay a Frankenstein monster dummy. Standing in front of the operating table, hovering over the Frankenstein monster, was a doctor. It looked like a dummy also. But as they entered the room, the doctor turned to face them and let out a chilling scream. At the same time, the Frankenstein creature sat on the bed. Kevin and Anna were paralyzed with fear, the type of fear you feel in the pit of your stomach and makes your blood run cold. Houdini jumped from Anna's hand, heading for the door as fast as his paws could carry him. Kevin and Anna followed right after.

Once outside, after catching their breath, they laughed.

"Wow! That was so cool!"

"It was awesome! You want to go again?"

"No, thanks. I think I'm good. You can go in if you want to. I'll stay out here. I have to look for Houdini," said Anna, looking through the bushes. "Hey, kitty, hey, kitty-kitty." *What is she doing?* she thought to herself. The cat knew his name. He always came when she called him. "Houdini, Houdini!" she called.

There were so many people. With all the people walking on the streets and between the cars driving by and with the loud music playing from the houses and cars, Houdini must've been really scared. *They don't call them scaredy-cat for no reason,* she thought. She had to find him fast, or he would keep on running. She continued to call the cat, walking behind houses and checking every bush. But Houdini was nowhere to be found.

"Anna!" said Kevin, catching up to her. "Oh my gosh! You should've gone with me. It was even better the second time. I think the doctor is a real person. He got out of the chair this time and tried to chase me. It was so awesome!"

"Kev, I'm worried. I can't find Houdini any-where. Please help me find him. He is probably really scared by now."

They both looked for the cat. They even recruited some of their friends to help them find him, but nothing. The cat seemed to have disappeared. It was about 10:00 p.m. by now, and they had to give up the search and return home without the cat. They would look again tomorrow. "It should be easier in the daylight and without all those people walking around," said Anna's mom while driving home.

Anna couldn't hold back the tears. He was out there all alone. The cat had never been out of the house except for today. "What if it got run over by a car or something?" she cried.

"Oh, honey, don't cry. I'm sure we'll find him tomorrow. You'll see. Your brother and I will help you make flyers and post them around. Someone will see him. I'm sure he'll turn out."

Anna couldn't sleep that night in spite of what her mother had said. She was still worried. She missed the cat being next to her. She missed the warmth of its body next to hers. Her bed felt really big without him, she thought as tears rolled from her eyes into the pillow.

*****

The next morning she woke up to the sound of the alarm clock. She was confused for a moment. She reached out for Houdini, and then she remembered. She had set the alarm for an earlier time so they could go out and put the flyer around the neighborhood before going to school; she wanted the cat to be found soon.

After breakfast her mom drove them around the neighborhood to get the flyers up. They took turns getting off the car to tape the flyers to the telephone poles. They were lucky they had a recent picture of the cat. Her mom had taken it yesterday, right before going to the festival. It was a picture of the three of them in their Halloween costumes. Kevin had cropped the picture in the computer, and only Houdini was showing. Someone would recognize him, she hoped.

That day the school day seemed to go on forever. She couldn't wait to get home. The school bus dropped her off about half a mile away as usual. As they approached the house, both of them ran to the house, hoping to find the cat there.

She heard stories before about cats that had been separate from their owners and had walked long distances to get back, sometimes across state lines. Maybe he was back.

When they approached the house, Anna's heart sank. She was expecting to see the cat in the front porch. But nothing. It wasn't there.

She rushed inside to call her mom at work. Maybe someone had seen the flyer and called her mom about Houdini. She grabbed the house phone from the kitchen wall and dialed her mom's number.

"Mom. Did you hear anything about Houdini? Did anyone call?"

"No, nothing yet, honey. I just checked my cell phone about five minutes ago, and there were no calls."

"Oh my gosh, Mom. He is not here either. What if something happened to him? There's lots of snakes here and hawks. What if a hawk took him?" Being in a rural area, she had heard a story about one of the residents who had seen a hawk take their small Yorkies from their backyard. "What if—"

"Anna honey, I'm really busy here. We will talk when I get back tonight. I will call if I hear anything, okay? Don't worry, honey. He'll be fine. I got to let you go now. Love you."

Houdini wasn't back that day or the next or the day after. It had been close to two weeks since the Halloween festival. No one called the number on the flyer. The flyers had withered and faded on the telephone poles, and Houdini was still gone.

Anna's heart was broken. She had nightmares almost every night about Houdini. She dreamed once that the cat was killed by a snake. She had woken up screaming and sweating profusely. Another time she saw him in her dreams wandering the fields, skinny and dirty, looking for food and water. She blamed herself for Houdini's disappearance. If only she had left him at home that day, that wouldn't have happened, and Houdini would still be there.

Even when she was awake, it was hard to keep Houdini off her mind. She loved that cat; they all did. The cat was part of the family.

Her mom had offered to get her another cat because she couldn't stand to see her so sad, but she had refused the offer. How do you replace your best friend? No cat would ever replace Houdini. She knew that, so why even try?

Chapter 4

Today was Kevin's birthday. He was turning fifteen. It was now November. The weather was cold, and the trees were mostly bare. Kevin wanted to have his birthday celebration at the laser tag. Whatever place they chose had to be inside because the temperature outside was very cold this time of year. Anna wondered about Houdini alone and cold out there. The thought of Houdini never escaped her mind.

They had come home late from the laser tag. Some of Kevin's close friends had come home with them. They were planning to watch a scary movie, have a bonfire in the backyard, and make s'mores.

By the time everyone left the house, it was almost 12:00 a.m. They didn't have to worry about school the following day; tomorrow was Sunday. But it had been a very long day, and they were all exhausted by the time they went to bed.

Anna woke up in the middle of the night and sat on her bed. Was she having a nightmare again? She was confused and disoriented when she heard a noise coming from downstairs. She waited to make sure it wasn't her imagination playing a trick on her.

When she heard it again, it sounded like footsteps. Who could be downstairs this late at night? Maybe it was Kevin on his way to the basement to play Xbox again. But for some reason, she had a very uneasy feeling about this. What if someone broke into the house? she was thinking when she heard the TV come on. Her heart started to raise, and her hands were sweaty and shaking. She had to find out, she thought.

Trying very hard not to make any noise, she opened the door to her room and walked very slowly to her mom's room adjacent to hers. The upstairs of the house had wooden floors, and the footsteps could be heard from downstairs easily, so she had to walk very softly.

She walked straight to her mom's room. The door was closed but not locked. So she turned the doorknob quietly and walked in.

"Mom! Mom! Wake up! I think there is someone downstairs," she whispered. "I heard footsteps. Mom! Wake up!"

"What? What?" she said, half asleep.

"Mom, there is someone in the house, I think. I heard noises coming from downstairs, footsteps. We have to check."

"Honey, it's probably Kevin. Did you check his room?"

"No," she whispered.

Mrs. Wellington got up without making a lot of noise, and they walked together to Kevin's room.

They were expecting to see an empty bed. But to their surprise, Kevin was in his bed, sound asleep.

"Oh no! Mom, I told you! Should we wake Kevin up?"

"Kev, Kev. Wake up."

Kevin sat up on the bed, making the bed squeak. "What?"

"We think there is someone in the house," they whispered. "We heard noises, footsteps."

"K, Mom, I'll go with you," said Kevin, grabbing a baseball bat from his closet. "Give Anna the cell phone. She can call 911."

They both walked down the stairs, trying very hard not be heard. Halfway down the stairs, they peeked through the stair spindles into the family room, where the noises had come from. They had a good view of the family room from there.

They froze with fear. Sitting on the sofa with his back to them, they saw the figure of a person wearing a black hoodie. They both panicked. They were stricken with fear so bad they could hardly move.

"Anna, call 911!" her mom yelled from the stairs.

Both Mom and Kevin rushed to the family room. Kevin, bat in hand, was ready to strike, when the figure turned around and yelled, "No. Please! Don't! It's me, Houdini."

Anna's mom turned on the light. And standing in front of them was a boy, a teenager about fifteen years old. He was about five feet six inches in stature, slim but muscular. He had fair skin. His hair was very black and spiked. But his face's most striking feature was his eyes. They were big, almond shaped, and very green in color; they looked almost… fluorescent.

"No, you're not," screamed Kevin. "You better start talking, and you better start talking soon, dude. The police are on their way."

"It's me! It's me! I swear. I can explain. Please, just put the bat down."

A lot of thoughts were going through their heads. This guy didn't look menacing, and he wasn't armed. But he sure had to be crazy. How could he be Houdini? Houdini was a cat, and how did he know about the cat anyway?

They had never seen this guy before.

"Let's all calm down please," the boy pleaded. "I can explain, sort of…" Within a few seconds, Houdini saw Kevin charging at him. "Ahhhhhhh!" Kevin was swinging the bat at the boy but missed every time. The boy was too quick for him. His reflexes were too sharp.

Anna was in the family room now and stared at the boy with big open eyes and unable to speak a word. Her mom was staring at them, not knowing what to do, speechless too, it seemed.

"Stop please!" he repeated as he jumped with ease, trying to evade Kevin's moves. "Please put the bat down. I can explain, just listen please."

Kevin stopped eventually, heavily panting.

"Let me explain please!" the kid pleaded again.

Kevin stood still, out of breath. The boy began to explain.

"I don't remember much, but I remember running. I remember being scared. And running, running fast for a long while, and then I guess I blacked out. When I came to again, I was in an abandoned dilapidated barn. I've never seen this place before. I was scared and confused. I was also naked. I looked around the barn for something to cover myself with. I found an old blanket discarded in a corner of the barn, and I wrapped myself in it. I stepped out of the barn. I saw a house close by, and I walked to it, not knowing what else to do. I was in a daze. I looked into the window. I saw no one inside, so I checked the side door to see if it would open. It was closed. I then went around checking all the windows until I found one that was unlocked. I climbed through it into the house. It didn't look like anyone lived there. There were a couple of pieces of furniture, a chair, an old mattress, pots and pans scattered over the kitchen counter, and that sort of thing. It looked like the house was abandoned for quite a while. And…"

Suddenly the interior of their house was illuminated with red and blue light. They heard a knock on the door. "Police, open up!"

Anna's mom went to the front door and opened it, and right in front of her stood two police officers.

"We got a call from this residence about a break-in. Is everything all right?" one of them said while he pointed the flashlight into the house.

They all looked at each other. The boy's eyes were big with fear.

"Yes, everything's all right, Officer. False alarm, I'm afraid. It turned out to be nothing. Must've been a raccoon."

"Do you mind if we go in and take a look just to make sure?" the officer asked.

"Sure, go right ahead. We were just getting ready to go back to bed," said Anna's mom.

The officer stepped inside and looked around. "Are these your kids, ma'am?"

The boy looked at Kevin and then at Mrs. Wellington with pleading eyes.

"Yes, this is my son and daughter, and he is just a friend of my son who's having a sleepover," she said, pointing at Houdini. "Like I said, everything is all right. Sorry we didn't call back to explain. I really appreciate you guys coming all the way out here."

"Oh, don't worry, ma'am. It's our job. I'm glad everything's all right. Good evening, ma'am," said the officer, walking out the door and closing the door behind them.

"Keep talking," said Kevin, looking at the boy with suspicion in his eyes and raising the bat again.

"Where was I?" said the boy as he let out a sigh of relief. "Oh yeah, I looked around and found some discarded articles of clothing in the bedroom closet. Among them a pair of jeans, a pair of work boots, and this black sweatshirt. I didn't know who I was or how I had gotten there. My brain was in a fog. I was too afraid to leave the house, too afraid to do anything. I found some cans of food in the kitchen drawers, and that is how I survived for days. Eventually I started to recall things. First, the Halloween festival, the haunted house, Anna," he said, looking straight at her. "Every day I remember a little more… but I couldn't make sense of any of it. A house, a family, a cage… not knowing what to make of all that was happening, I went back to the barn to see if anything would jot my memory.

"I was looking for something. And there on the floor of the barn, I saw it. Right on the hay was the collar. I picked it up and looked at it. It read Houdini on the front of it, and this address was engraved on the back of the cat's collar. I knew I had to find the house. I remember the house vaguely, but I didn't know in what direction to go. It took me a whole day to find this address. I had to stop at a couple of houses along the way to get directions. When I got here, I didn't know what house it was. I went to the main house first. When I looked through the window, I did not recognize the place. So I came to this one. I knew this one had to be the one. I remembered the kitchen and the family room. I remembered watching TV sitting on this sofa. So I knew this was home. I waited for everyone to be asleep and got in through the kitchen window. I was thinking about a way to show myself to all of you when you came down the stairs, and the rest is history."

They were still trying to make sense of what they were hearing. How could this be? It was impossible. Who was this guy? And what was the purpose of all this?

Was this for real? Was this boy standing in front of them actually the cat? The thought was blowing their mind.

Sitting in the family room, they stayed up all night talking. They asked him all kinds of questions to prove that what he said was true. The boy described Anna's room on the second floor to a tee, from the bedspread on her bed to the blue cat tower and scratching pole she had bought him. There was no way he had seen her room. She always kept the door looked when she wasn't home. She had asked for a lock on her bedroom door. She liked to lock herself in the room whenever she was alone in the house; it made her feel safe. They knew the second floor was too high for anyone to look through the windows. There was no possible way for the boy to know any of this. He knew about movies that he and Anna had watched together.

He recalled conversations the family had in this very kitchen with no one around but them. He described the haunted house, the doctor, the cages, the Halloween festival, etc. He remembered his life with them, but nothing from before. He didn't know who he was or how he came to be.

It was five in the morning by the time they went to bed. Houdini was to sleep on the sofa. They would continue this conversation tomorrow.

Mrs. Wellington was alone in her room. It was past six in the morning; she knew she needed her rest. She was working the morning shift at the diner tomorrow, or today really, but she could not fall asleep. The events of the last day were weighting heavily in her mind. It was all so incredible, so unexpected. She kept going back over the conversation she had with Houdini (the cat). Even saying it made no sense to her. It was really hard to believe, but the boy's story was tugging at her heart. A kid alone in the world, not knowing who he was or how he got there—it was an awful story but one that she knew too well, one that she could relate to. She had been an orphan too all her life. She had spent her childhood just jumping from one foster home after another, not belonging anywhere or having anyone to call her own, until she turned eighteen and exited out of the system.

Because of it, she had never known what if felt like to be part of a family or even look in the eyes of someone that looked like herself. Not until she met Mr. Wellington and made a family of her own. Houdini's situation broke her heart. It woke up feelings she didn't know she had, feelings of empathy, maternal instincts, and an overwhelming need to protect him. Her life had been a lonely life that she didn't want or ask for. She had cried herself to sleep as a little girl too many times to count. But she was going to make sure that Houdini's life would be different, that he would always have a family to call his own and a home to come back to. The thought of it made her smile. She would be Houdini's mom; she was going to make a difference.

Her eyes felt heavy with sleep, but the smile remained on her face as she drifted into sleep.

Chapter 5

The following morning, sitting at the kitchen table, the four of them discussed many important things and made lots of plans. They talked a very long time. They didn't know how all this had come to be or if this was even possible, but if Houdini was going to be part of the family, they had to find a way to explain him to people.

He needed documentation, he needed to go to school, and most importantly, they had to find out about him. Where had he come from? How was this all possible? Who was this boy?

Houdini asked to see a picture of the cat he used to be and stared at it for hours. He didn't remember being a cat.

Anna had mixed feelings about what was happening. On the one hand she was happy that Houdini was back, but on the other hand, was he really back? She didn't have a cat anymore. This new boy would be more like a brother to her now. And he looked to be Kevin's age or a little older. He probably wouldn't want to spend time with her either. She felt a little sad; she had lost her best friend.

Anna's mom decided she would go back to the Humane Society to find out anything she could find about the strange cat they had adopted and its origin. There had to be a logical explanation to all this. Houdini was going with her. Maybe seeing the place he was adopted from would help him remember something about himself, anything really. He was desperate for information; he needed to know who he was.

As they walked in the building, Anna's mom spotted the lady that had helped her last time.

"Hi, I don't know if you remember me, but my daughter and I were here a while back—"

"Of course I remember," interrupted the clerk. "Mrs. Wellington. Isn't it? You adopted Houdini. How can I forget. He was a legend around here." She laughed. "How is he doing?"

"Oh, he is doing fine. We are really happy to have him, but I was just wondering if there was anything else you remember about him."

"What do you mean?"

"Let say, did anyone see who dropped him off? You mentioned you have cameras on the outside of the store. Did you watch the tape?"

"We did, the next morning. Nothing out of the ordinary. A man dropped it off. We noticed he was very careful not to look at the camera. But I guess that's pretty normal when you are doing something you're not supposed to do."

"Anything that may have happened when he was here? Anything that comes to mind?"

"Well, I know he didn't like the vet. He was fine with all the other personnel, but he cowered and whimpered in his cage whenever the vet tried to examine him. He even jumped at him once and scratched his face. Why, is there any problem with the cat?"

"No, no, like I said, we are very happy with him. Just curiosity, I guess. We just came here to schedule his shots, and I thought I would ask, that's all. I see you guys are very busy, so I think I'll just call and make an appointment over the phone."

They were ready to exit the store when the lady said, "Wait a minute please. I just remember I got something you may want." She opened the bottom drawer of her desk, and from under a bunch of files, she took out a cat's collar. "The cat was wearing this when we found him. We don't know what it means, but maybe you should have it."

Back in the house they continued to examine the collar. That's all Houdini had been doing in the ride back from the store.

The collar was metallic, not leather like most cats' collar. The metal was silver in tone and very glossy. They weren't sure about the material it was made of. There was some type of medallion dangling from it. The medallion had a symbol they had never seen before. And on the reverse of the metal collar, the name Adam was engraved followed by the number 2008.

Adam, he pondered. *And 2008. What could that mean? Could it be the year I was born? That would make me about ten years old. I am older, I look older. Fifteen, maybe sixteen,* he thought. *And who had named me Adam? Adam, Adam,* he repeated. It didn't ring a bell. But he knew he liked the name Houdini better; the name Adam meant nothing to him.

Mrs. Wellington had gotten on the internet. She was trying to find a way to explain Houdini's presence, when she came across an article that called her attention, the immigrant student's right to attend school.

According to the article, the US Supreme Court ruled in *Plyler v. Doe* (457 US 202 [1982]) that undocumented children had the same right to attend public school as any other children. Student without a social security number should be assigned a number generated by the school without any questions asked.

She could not believe her luck. Right in front of her was the answer to their problem.

That was exactly what she would do, she decided. She would register Houdini at school as an illegal immigrant, and no one would be the wiser.

It was the night before school started for Houdini. He was now Houdini Wellington, an illegal immigrant according to the school records. But those records were confidential. No one would know about this information. Kevin and Houdini were going to attend the same school. Kevin would tell his friends Houdini was his cousin who had come to live with their family. They had decided that the less people knew, the better.

Kevin and Houdini shared bunkbeds in Kevin's room now, and most of his clothes. He had gotten new clothes too. But he wore the black hoodie over everything. It was part of his identity. He felt like not having a known identity. He tried very hard to establish one. After seeing the cat's picture, he had asked Anna for some white acrylic paint and had drawn an upside-down triangle on the front of his black hoodie, a triangle just like the one he had seen on the cat's chest. Doing this made him feel better, like he was repossessing a part of his identity, of his essence. Yeah, he thought, looking at himself in the mirror. He was Houdini Wellington, the new student at Jackson High.

Houdini was very nervous about going to school. If he had ever attended school, he didn't remember. He was grateful that he was able to sit next to Kevin on the bus ride. But he still felt butterflies in his stomach as they approached the school.

Jackson High was the only high school in their small town. There was only one middle school too, Jackson Middle. The school was a big old brick building with a lot of historic charm. It was a big school for such small town, but since it was the only school for miles, the kids from all the adjacent towns attended the school too.

He was glad he had Kevin to navigate him to his classrooms. Throughout the day he had to stand in front of every classroom and introduce himself as the new kid. So far, he used the speech they had rehearsed at home. He was Houdini Wellington. He was originally from Ohio. He was here living with relatives, etc. Most kids didn't even bother to look up to see who was talking. Then the teacher would assign him a seat, and that was it, except for his third period—math class. When he introduced himself as Houdini, he heard a voice from the back of the classroom.

"Dude, what kind of stupid name is that?"

Houdini looked up to see a big husky boy sitting in the back of the classroom against the wall. He was wearing a black leather jacket. And his hair looked unkept and oily. He had a big smirk on his face.

"Keith! I think that's enough," said the teacher. "Houdini, please take a seat. We are very happy to have you with us this school year."

Classes went on without a hitch. He was surprised to know that he knew the subjects.

At lunchtime he entered the cafeteria, looking for Kevin. He was hoping they had the same lunch period. He did not see him anywhere.

So he decided to go to the library instead. He wasn't hungry anyway, and he needed to find any information he could find on the symbol he had seen on the cat's original collar. It had to mean something, and he needed to figure it out.

"Did you go find out anything about the cat's whereabouts?" asked a man of about fifty, slim and tall with salt-and-pepper hair. "We need to find the cat as soon as possible. The police are on our tails."

"No, nothing so far," said a man sitting across from him in what seemed to be an abandoned warehouse. "I went back to the Humane Society once more today, trying to see if the cat was still there. And he was not. I left as quick as possible. I didn't want to raise suspicion. I know they sometimes use foster homes to house the animals while waiting for the cats to get adopted," said the man.

"But that could be a number of homes. It would take a while before we get hold of that information."

"We are working on it. One of our men just applied to be a volunteer at the shelter. It won't be long before we'll get the information we need."

"I sure hope you're right. We are running out of time. We need to recover that collar. That's the only thing that would implicate us in any way. The only piece of evidence… hopefully, we'll find it before the police do. Forgetting to remove it from the cat was a grave mistake."

"Don't worry about it, boss. We will follow any lead we can find. We will retrieve that collar. It's just a matter of time now."

"But time is running out. We can't afford to make any mistakes now. Everything's is a stake."

Houdini entered the school library. It was a library like many others. There were a number of aisles full of books. There was a desk in the middle of the room. A librarian stood behind the counter. And there was a glass-enclosed computer room to the right. There weren't many kids in the library now, only a handful of them, most of them sitting by themselves, minding their own business. He walked straight to the counter.

"Is there anything I can help you with?" said the librarian, an elderly lady wearing glasses.

"I need to see if I can find books on signs."

"What kind of signs? We have quite a selection of astrology book in the science section."

"No, no that type of sign. It's more like a symbol, I guess, not signs. My bad."

"Historical symbol? Mythological symbol?"

"I really don't know… I found a symbol in one of the books I am reading, and I'm trying to find the meaning of it," Houdini lied.

"If we have any books on the subject, it would be on our medical section. Have you tried the internet? Nowadays one can find information about almost anything in the internet. Faster too," said the lady.

"Yes, thanks. You're right," said Houdini, walking toward the computer room.

He sat down at the computer but didn't have the slightest idea of what to look for. Where should he start? The collar was an enigma to him.

He finally keyed in the word *symbols*. A lot of information came up on the computer screen. A lot of web addresses: symbol copy-paste character.com, images of symbol. There were hundreds of symbols. He didn't recognize any of them. At the bottom of the page, it read "More images of symbols." He clicked it and more symbols appeared. It was going to take him a very long time to go through all of them.

Next Wikipedia—the Free Encyclopedia gave the definition of *symbol.* Not what he was looking for, he thought. Symbols.com was about zodiac; there was another address about Facebook symbols.

The list went on and on: Celtic symbols, Greek symbols, animal symbolism, etc. He was getting real frustrated when someone spoke to him from the door.

"Hey! Do you know what time it is? Everyone is back to class. Do you have a pass?"

"What? No. I lost track of time, I guess," he said, getting up and walking toward the door. He looked at his schedule, trying to find his next class.

"Are you new? Can I help you find your class-room?" asked the boy. "By the way, my name is Jake," said the boy, extending his hand to Houdini.

"Nice to meet you," said Houdini, shaking his hand.

Houdini followed the boy's directions to his classroom. He was ten minutes late. He didn't have to introduce himself to the classroom this time since the class was already in progress. But the teacher was sure to mention that tardiness was not tolerated in his class, and next time he would get after-school detention. Houdini found an empty seat at the back of the classroom and sat down. They were playing a movie in class, so he tried to keep himself from falling asleep.

The first day of school was over. He spotted Kevin on his way to the bus. Luckily, he had remembered the bus number. He saw Kevin at a distance; he was talking with a group of friends.

"Hey, Houdini, this way," called Kevin.

Houdini approached the group. Kevin introduced him to some of his friends as his cousin Houdini. They all said their names. Kevin was in the middle of introducing yet another of his friends when the boy said, "Yes, Houdini, I know. We meet earlier today. Nice to see you again."

Houdini looked up and recognized the boy from the library smiling at him. "Yes, we met earlier. Jake, isn't it?"

They all jumped in the school bus. The boys were horseplaying and laughing on the ride back home. Houdini was quiet; he kept staring out the window. It was mostly empty fields. Every now and then they would pass a house. Some of the houses had horses either on the front or to the side of the house. There were also some cows on the field, barns, etc. Some of the houses were hidden in some areas, but you could tell by the mailboxes on the side of the road that there were houses down that road.

His mind kept going back to the symbols he had seen on the internet. He had his work cut out for him, he thought. This would take weeks, even months, to figure all of this out.

The bus kept stopping to drop off kids. Their stop was one of the last ones. The bus was almost empty when it finally stopped for them to get out. They sat on a big boulder on the side of the road. They were supposed to wait for Anna's bus to drop her off so they could walk home together. It was a long stretch to the house.

"Hey, Kev," said Houdini, "how about your friend Jake?"

"What about him?"

"He seems to be a nice guy. He helped me get to one of my classes today. You know him long?"

"Yeah, we went to the same elementary school. We had some classes together, not a lot. He is a little odd. People used to tease him a lot. I think he has some type of autism, I'm not sure. But he is an okay guy. Smart too."

Anna's bus stopped, and they walked together home. They had to pass a few homes on the way to their house. Most of the houses were sat on an acre or acre and a half and were fenced with chicken wire to keep animals from escaping. Some houses had dogs that ran free behind the fence, following them and barking all the way to the next property fence and continuing to bark as they walked away. All the dogs seemed to be very irritated by Houdini's presence. They ran from one end of the property to the other, barking viciously at him. At times it looked as if they were going to jump the fence and attack him. Kevin and Anna had never seen those dogs so out of control.

That night at supper, the conversation was all about Houdini.

"How was your first day of school?" Mrs. Wellington asked.

"Good, I got lost a couple of times. Other than that, it was all good."

"Did anyone ask where you were from?"

"Yeah, I told them from Ohio, like we agreed upon."

"Anyone questioned?"

"No, no one I could tell. Most kids didn't even pay attention."

"Mom, you should've seen the neighborhood dogs on the way here. They wanted to kill Houdini," said Anna, laughing. "It was so funny."

"Funny and scary," said Kevin. "I was getting ready to run. Houdini made a new friend though."

"Not a friend. He just seems nice, that's all."

That night Houdini had a nightmare. In his dream he saw himself as a boy, not a cat. He was in some type of laboratory. He was surrounded by doctors wearing white coats. But he could not see their faces. He was hooked to machines that monitored his body reactions to different things. He was afraid, very afraid. They were drawing blood out of him. He did not know what was coming next, but he knew that he wouldn't like it. He woke up screaming. He woke Kevin up.

"Are you okay?" asked Kevin, half asleep.

"Yes, I guess. I had a bad dream, that's all. Go back to bed, it's okay."

It took Houdini a while to be able to fall asleep again. He couldn't get the images out of his mind. Was it a dream? Or was he remembering something from his past? What could that mean? Who were these people? Were they even real or a figment of his imagination? He didn't know what to make of it.

When he went back to bed, he dreamed he was a cat again. This time he was in the same lab. But he was locked up in a cage. This time there was no one around; he was alone. The lights were off, it was dark, but he could see very well in the dark. There were other cages on the other side of the room. He was trying very hard to see through the bars of the cage. He was about to see what was in them when he woke up again, sweating and panting. It was going to be a long night, he thought, still shaking with fear.

The next day in school, he was exhausted. He had hardly slept the night before. He was having a hard time keeping up with what was going on in his classes. He was too tired. He finally fell asleep in his math class.

He had fallen asleep for about ten minutes, it felt like, he wasn't sure, when he had a rude awakening. Someone kicked his chair. The impact and the loud noise woke him up.

"Hey, dude, are you homeless or something? By the way, you were drooling. That's disgusting."

He was trying to understand what was happening when he heard a girl's voice coming from a desk next to his, "Hey! Leave him alone. What? Does it make you feel better to pick on people? Mind your own business, would you?"

He looked up to see the same guy from the day before, and confronting him was a girl. But not just a girl. A beautiful girl, he thought.

She had long brown hair and green eyes.

"Whatever," said Keith, slowly returning back to his seat in the back of the classroom.

Houdini sat back on his chair, trying to hide his embarrassment. But he could feel his face turning red as everyone turned to look at him.

He was the first one out of class when the bell rang. He waited by the door until he saw the girl come out of the classroom. And he tried to catch up to her.

"Hey, thank you for coming to my rescue earlier. That was nice, what you did."

"Oh, don't worry about it. He's just a jerk. He likes to pick on people. Don't let it bother you."

"I'll try… By the way, my name is Houdini. What's yours?"

"Krissy. Well, Kristina really, but my friends call me Krissy."

"Well, nice to meet you, Krissy. See you around?"

"Sure," she said, rushing to her locker to meet a girlfriend.

He met Kevin and his friends for lunch. They all sat at the same table. He decided not to go to the library today; he might fall asleep and be late for class again. Last thing he needed was an after-school detention. Kevin and he were engaged in a conversation when he saw her again. Standing in the lunch line was Krissy. She was too busy talking to some friend to even notice him. But he could see her well.

He was trying to follow the conversation the guys were having, trying to look interested. But his eyes kept following Krissy.

Kevin followed Houdini's eyes to see what he was staring at.

"What you looking at, bro? Krissy?"

"You know her too?"

"It's a small town. Everybody knows everybody. Why? do you like her?"

"She is my math class. We spoke briefly today. She's beautiful though."

"Yeah, she is, but she is also president of the school paper. She plays in the lacrosse team and is one of the most popular girls in school. No offense, bro. But way out of your league."

"Maybe... How do you feel about lacrosse? Been to any good games this year?"

"Suit yourself, bro. Good luck with that."

Chapter 6

It had been raining lately, and the temperature was very cold, but no snow yet. It should've been snowing by now. Thanksgiving break was just around the corner. Houdini was getting used to the school routine, and he was making good grades even though some of the teachers had complaints about him being too jumpy. One time during class, a stapler fell from the teacher's desk, scaring Houdini, who ran for the door for dear life. He was also fidgety and easily distracted. Any noise would get his attention. All signs of attention deficit disorder, the teachers claimed. They had even scheduled a conference with "his aunt" and tried to persuade her to have him tested for ADD.

He was still having nightmares occasionally. It was always the same—the mysterious lab, the faceless doctors—but regardless of how many nightmares he had, he wasn't any closer to finding out who he was or where he came from.

He had tried a couple more times to go in the internet and try to find the meaning of the symbol he had seen on the cat's collar. Jake was helping him now. He was really good with computers. The last couple of times Houdini visited the library, Jake had been there. He told Houdini that he'd rather go to the library during lunch; he had a hard time socializing and making friends, and he preferred to be alone anyway. Houdini told him what he was trying to find in the internet without giving away any information on the real reason behind his search.

Jake offered to help Houdini find the meaning of the symbol, but even with Jake's help, he found nothing. So he had put the search on the back burner for now. It would come to him, he thought; it was just a matter of time.

In spite of Kevin's opinion, he and Krissy had become friends lately. He had made sure to show up at her lacrosse games, dragging Kevin with him every time. The first time he went, she was surprised to see him at the game. But later she kind of expected to see him there. He spotted her looking for him in the crowd a couple of times. When their eyes met, she looked away embarrassed. It gave Houdini hope.

He was going to do anything possible to get her to like him. She was the first thing he thought of every day when he woke up in the morning. Once, he pretended that he had forgotten his math book at home, and she offered to share her book with him. He would do anything to be close to her. He waited for her sometimes after class and found all kinds of excuses to talk to her and walk her to her next class. She had even come to his rescue once more when Keith had made fun of his black sweatshirt. He had accused him of wearing the same shirt all the time and having no sense of style, which brought up a conversation about it with Krissy.

That day they sat together at lunch, and she asked questions about him.

"I don't know what this guy has against you," she said. "It's not like he's so stylish himself. He wears the same leather jacket too all the time. Did you know him from before? Did anything happen between you two?"

"Nope, never seen him before in my life. Don't know what his problem is, really. I'm just trying to stay out of trouble, but he is beginning to get on my nerves."

"Well, you have to admit that you have an unusual name. Who are you named after?"

"No one in my family. My dad was really into magic, so he named me Houdini after the world's most famous magician, Harry Houdini, the greatest escape artist ever known," Houdini lied puffing his chest out, making her laugh.

"Are you into magic too?"

"No, but my cousin is or *was* at one point."

"Okay, last question, I promise. What's up with the black hoodie? Does it mean something too?"

"Nah. Just like it, that's all. It's kind of my security blanket. I guess. Makes me feel safe, and every superhero needs a trademark." He smiled. "Besides, black makes me look sexy," he said, winking and bumping his shoulder against hers.

Krissy looked down at the floor and smiled.

"K, my turn to ask the questions. Would you like to go to the movies with me? This Friday."

Krissy looked at him, their eyes locking. In the bright light of the cafeteria, she looked very pretty, he thought. Krissy could see his big green eyes staring back at her, hopeful. He was very handsome, she thought, funny too. And she loved his crooked smile.

"Sure," she said. "I got to ask my mom, but my friend Stacey got to come with me, I'm almost sure. My parents won't let me go alone. Is that okay with you?"

"Sure," he said, trying to act casual and conceal his happiness.

John had been volunteering at the Humane Society for about a week now. He was running out of patience. Finding the cat had proven to be harder than he ever thought. The adoption records were in the file cabinets in the main office. Volunteers didn't have a reason to go in there, especially when his job consisted of cleaning the cages and feeding the animals. What reason would he have to inquire about adoption records? He did not want to raise any suspicious about his motive for volunteering. He was beginning to think that if he wanted to get the information, he would have to break into the building at night, but that would prove to be hard. He had seen the cameras outside the building when he had dropped the cat, and he knew that they watched those videos every day.

Something had to be done, he thought. They were running out of time.

He was lost in thought, sitting in the employee's lunch room, when he overheard a couple of teenager talking.

"Hey, dude. Remember that freaky cat that used to be here? He was a riot. I kind of miss him. Nothing really happens around here anymore. If it wasn't because I need my community hour for school, I will ditch this place. I'm bored out of my mind."

"Yeah, that was a funny cat. Hilarious! I wonder what happened to him."

"Last time I heard, someone adopted him right around October, I think. When I came back after Halloween, he was already gone. Some family had adopted him, the Wellingtons. I overheard the clerk tell someone once. I'm not sure. Dude, remember when he…"

John had stopped listening. Could that be the cat? It had to be. He couldn't believe his luck. Finally he was on to something.

They weren't worried about the cat. The cat was a cat, that's all. They had gone to great lengths to make sure he didn't remember a thing. And even if he did, cats didn't talk, and even if it did, who in their right mind would believe something as crazy as that? No, the cat was not a problem. But the police had come snooping around a couple of times. They were getting too close, and it was only a matter of time before they were found out. The collar was the biggest piece of the puzzle. Without it, the police had no case, no proof of anything. But the collar was out there. Someone had it. And they needed to have it back.

The Wellington family, huh? I will look in the Yellow Pages, he thought. *It is a small town. How many families can there be with that last name?*

His volunteer days were over now.

Houdini had gotten out of school that day. He couldn't believe his good fortune. Krissy had said yes about going to the movies with him next Friday. Maybe she was warming up to him. On the bus ride home from school, he kept daydreaming about her. He would have to find a friend to double-date with Stacey. Maybe Kevin or Jake, but Jake was shy, and he didn't know how any of them felt about Stacey. He would have to ask one of them. The bus came to a stop, and Kevin and he got out. They did not have to wait for Anna. She was home with the flu. And she had missed school. They were walking home, goofing around and talking about school. They were passing the houses along the way. The dogs were acting as crazy as ever. They always did when Houdini passed by. He was used to it by now. He got the same reaction from dogs wherever he went. But this time, one of the dogs, a pit bull, got loose from one of the houses. It jumped the fence and started to chase them. They took off running as fast as they could with the dog after them. This dog was vicious. They were running fast, but the dog kept gaining distance. Kevin wasn't as fast as he was. But the dog wasn't interested in Kevin. So after Kevin stopped on the side of the road, out of breath and too tired, the dog kept chasing Houdini. The dog was fast, and it was close. Houdini could feel the dog's breathing on the back of his legs.

Houdini's heart was pounding out of his chest. His legs were about to give out. He was panic-stricken. He was about to pass out with fear when he found himself on top of a tree. He looked down and saw the dog looking up, barking viciously at him, trying to climb the tree in an effort to get him, but he was out of reach now, and he was… he could not believe it—he was cat again! His fur was up and his back was arched; he was hissing back at the dog. The dog kept barking furiously at the tree, growling and scratching the trunk of the tree, trying to get to him.

Eventually, the dog lost interest and went back home, and Houdini got down from the tree, went into some bushes, and passed out. Kevin found him about an hour later and took him home.

As they walked home, Houdini's mind was racing. He was in a fog again. He remembered running from the dog. He remembered being up on the tree, trying to escape it. But he didn't know when or how he became a cat. And why or when he had passed out. By the time Kevin found him, he was human again.

He had to learn what triggered the change. The first time it happened, he was afraid and running away from the haunted house. And this time he had been afraid also… afraid for his life. Same scenario, he thought. Maybe it was the adrenaline his body released when he was afraid, or it was his accelerated heart rate that had triggered the change. He had no idea, but he knew he had no control over it. And that had to change. He had to learn to control it, or he would be found out. He had been lucky so far. There had been no one around the two times it had happened, he thought. There had to be a logical explanation to all this nonsense. And he had to get to bottom of it before someone other than his family found out about it. If this would come out, he would become a circus freak. He would be in every TV show, on the news, and on the tabloids, and scientists would be after him to study him. He would become a science experiment. They would take him away. And all his nightmares would come true. Whatever was happening to him had to remain a secret.

"Hey, Houdini, this is Krissy," said the voice on the phone. "How are you?"

"Good, what's up?"

"I was calling about the movies Friday night. My mom said it was okay to go as long as Stacey goes with us too."

"Cool, I'm thinking of asking Jake to go with us too. Are you okay with that?"

"I am… I guess. I don't know about Stacey though. I don't think she even knows him."

"Oh, he's all right. I am sure they'll get along."

"K, I'll let her know. My mom is driving us. I guess we'll meet you guys there? Around seven? The movie starts at seven thirty."

"What movie is that? We never discussed it."

"Oh, sorry, it's a scary movie. I hope you're not afraid," teased Krissy.

"Afraid? Me? Never."

Chapter 7

Houdini asked Jake to go to the movies with Krissy, Stacey, and him. Kevin had already made plans with his friends for that night. Houdini and Jake arrived at the town square early. The girls weren't there yet, so they decided to go into one of the stores that sold old vinyl records. Toward the back of the store, there was a section filled with old record players and vinyl albums. Houdini realized he liked '80s music, and he knew quite a lot about it too. He didn't know why, but he didn't question most things these days. Everything was a mystery. He didn't know anything about his past or even himself. His taste in music was the list of his problems. Jake liked the '80s music too, so they were looking through the albums, deciding what to buy. Houdini was sure he had seen one of the old record players in the basement at home.

"Hey, look at this one," said Jake, picking an album from the box and showing it to Houdini. "It's Guns N' and Roses' Appetite for Destruction I love this album, dude."

They were looking through the back of the record, looking at the song content. "'Sweet Child of Mine.' Cool. I like this one too." They kept looking through the albums and talking about different bands from the '80s. Houdini finally decided to buy the Album Van Halen, his favorite song running with the devil was feature in it.

They got out of the store singing the lyrics: "Running with the devil / hold on hold on / I'm running with the devil /ooh ooh / one more time." They were playing an air guitar solo, when they saw the girls coming in their direction. They both stopped in midair, turning red on the face.

The girls pretended they hadn't seen what happened but were trying hard not to laugh. After saying hi, they walked together to the theater. The movie was about to start. It was named *The Night of the Zombie Apocalypse*. The movie was rated R, so they decided to purchase tickets for a different movie, hide in the bathroom, and then sneak into the R-rated movie when no one was watching. The movie theater was full, it being a Friday night. They didn't find seats together, so Krissy and Houdini sat together and Stacey and Jake sat on the row behind them. The movie was very gory and scary. Through some of the scary scenes Stacey and Krissy would scream. And Houdini took the opportunity to hold Krissy close. Another scary scene came on, and Krissy screamed real loud.

They heard a voice coming from the back row, "Can you morons keep it down? We are trying to watch here."

They looked back to see where the voice was coming from, and they saw Keith standing up.

"What's your problem, bro?" replied Houdini.

"Oh, look who we have here. Houdini and Krissy. No wonder she is always defending you. Its Beauty and the Freak!"

"Listen, bro, I don't want any trouble. Let's just watch the movie, okay?" Houdini was trying very hard to control his temper. He was making a move toward Keith.

"Hey, don't listen to him. He is just a loser," said Krissy, holding him back.

"Loser? You are the loser going for him," he said, looking straight at Houdini. "Dude, you're a freak. What's wrong with your eyes?"

Houdini felt like he was losing control of his emotions. He was beginning to shake with anger, about to jump Keith, when one of the movie theater employees walked in to see what all the screaming was about. Houdini ran to the bathroom. He didn't know what was happening to him. He felt blood rushing to his head and his heartbeat racing. In the bathroom mirror, he could see his pupil. His eyes looked feline. Leaning against the bathroom sink, he took very deep and long breaths, trying to calm himself down, and a few minutes later, when he looked in the bathroom mirror again, he could see his pupils changing from vertical to normal.

He was about to change again, he thought with concern. He was relieved he was able to stop it in time. But he had to learn to control it. This was way too close; he had to be more careful.

When he went back to the theater, he realized that they had all been kicked out.

The three of them were waiting for him outside the movie theater. Krissy ran to him with concern on her voice. "Are you okay?" she asked.

"Yeah, I'm fine. What happened?"

"They realized we were in the wrong movie, so they kicked us out. We were lucky they didn't call our parents."

"Where is Keith?"

"He is gone. They told him to leave or they would call the police, so he split," said Jake.

"So what now?" They stood around looking at each other in awkward silence.

It was beginning to snow, the first snowfall of the season. So they all stood looking up at the sky. It was coming down hard now. The snowflakes were falling all over the town square. Krissy and Stacey were standing with their arms stretched out, looking up and trying to get the falling snow in the palm of their hands. Before they knew it, they were having a good time. All that had happened before was forgotten. Houdini put the hood of his black hoodie up to cover his head. They all did the same as they ran to the park across the street, laughing.

It was going to be a while before they were supposed to be picked up. So they sat on the swings and talked about school, about the movie, about bullies. Later Houdini and Krissy said they were going for a walk; it was snowing but much less now. Only snow flurries were falling. They were walking around the town square. There were plenty of people out that night. The pizza place was full. Almost every restaurant was full. There were people everywhere. They walked to the ice cream place.

The line was long, so they sat on a table while they waited their turn.

"So how do you like it here?" asked Krissy. "Very different from Ohio, is it?"

"What? Oh, Ohio. No, not so much. I'm from a small town too."

"Do you miss your family?"

"A little," said Houdini, relieved that she hadn't asked the name of the town. "It's just my mom, really. My dad passed away a few years ago, heart attack." Houdini lied.

"Wow, sorry, I didn't know."

"Thanks, I'm okay though. It's been a while."

"How come you came to live here?" she asked.

"Oh, I got into a couple of fights at school, and my mom overreacted and sent me here. She said I was hanging with the wrong crowd. She wanted to put distance between us, my supposed bad friends and I."

Houdini was making the stories up as he went along. He would have to tell Kevin when he got home so they could get their story straight. He didn't want to be caught in a lie. He didn't want to lie either, but what choice did he have? He didn't have a past like everyone else, and people always asked. He was glad when it was their turn to order the ice cream.

"Well, I'm glad you're here," said Krissy with a half smile.

"Me too. I'm liking it here."

They were getting out of the store, ice cream in hand, when the wind hit their face. The temperature had dropped a few degrees. They both looked at each other, turned around, and went back into the ice cream store.

"Maybe a hot soup would've been a better idea."

"You think?" said Houdini.

"Oh, really, whose idea was it to get the ice cream, huh?"

"Okay, guilty, you win this time. But don't get used to it. I'm usually right, you know."

"Yeah, whatever! You wish!"

They sat back on a table by the window, eating their ice cream and talking. They were having a great time. Krissy found Houdini to be very interesting. He wasn't like all the other boys she knew. There was something different about him. She didn't know what it was, but she knew she liked him.

Through the glass window, they could see the snow falling and accumulating on the windowsill. After they were done with the ice cream, they walked slowly on the way back to the park.

"Do you think Stacey and Jake are okay?"

"Yeah, I don't see why not. They seem to be getting along."

They were crossing the street, and Houdini took the opportunity to hold her had. He was very happy to see that she didn't take away.

By the time they got back to the park, they found Stacey and Jake still sitting on the swings.

"Hey, guys, check this out," said Houdini, throwing himself on the ground. Not so long after, they were all lying on the ground, making snow angels in the fresh-fallen snow.

Chapter 8

The next day he asked Jake to go to the public library with him. He needed to find the meaning of the symbol on the cat's collar, and he knew that Jake was really good with computers. But he needed to be smart about it. He couldn't let anyone including his friend know the real reason of his search. Mrs. Wellington dropped them off at the public library.

After showing their library cards and getting a password for the library's public computer, they tried finding the symbol on the internet, but after a while of searching the web, in vain, they sat by a table in the back of the library. They got as many books as they could on signs and symbols and started to look through the books. They had a big pile of books on the table.

"Okay, it's going to be a long day," said Houdini. "Let's see if we have any luck this time."

"Yeah, let's see... Bro, what's so important about this symbol anyway? Why are you so obsessed with it?"

"I'm not obsessed. I'm just curios, you know. It's like when you are trying to remember the name of a song or a name, it drives you crazy until you remember it. It's something like that, I guess."

"Where did you see this symbol again?"

"I'm not sure anymore. I think I saw it in a book once, and then I've been having dreams about it. I don't know, it's weird."

They kept looking through book after book.

"Hey, Jake, if you don't mind me asking, why do some people tease you at school? Not that you are the only one getting teased though. I have Keith on my case too."

"Oh, I have Asperger syndrome, which is a type of autism. It's the highest side of the autism spectrum, the most functional. But I still have a hard time relating to people in social circles, making friends, and reading social clues. I'm also a little clumsy. So you know how judgmental people can be when you're different. They think I'm odd."

"Yeah, I know how people can be," said Houdini.

"The good thing is that people with Asperger sometimes tend to be very smart at one subject or have one talent. I guess computers is my thing. Not too bad. Comes in handy sometimes."

"Yep," said Houdini, going over the pages of one book on historical symbol.

"Hey, do you have a picture of the symbol we are looking for? This drawing is not the best," said Jake, pointing at a piece of paper they had centered on top of the table between them.

"Just look for anything similar to that. I will know when I see it. It's hard to explain, but it's stuck in my head," said Houdini. But in his mind, he was thinking about the cat collar. It was hidden away in one of his desk drawers. Nobody but his family had seen it, and no one would until he got to the bottom of this. The engraving on the collar medal was hard to see; it was small. It consisted of a circle made of two different color lines. There was something in the middle of it he hadn't figured out yet, but he would recognize it if he would see it, he thought.

"Hey, Jake, what do you think of Stacey?"

"She is nice, I guess. We talked, a lot of awkward silence too, but I think she is all right. How about Krissy? You guys seem to be hitting it off."

"Yeah, she is great. We had a great time. Thanks for going with us though. I owe you one."

"It's all right," said Jake.

They spent hours going through different books, with no luck. They talked about other things too—school, girls, football. They had spent almost all afternoon in the library. So they decided to write down the name of the books they had already seen so they wouldn't waste time looking through them again the next time.

After dropping off Jake at his home, on the way home from the library, Houdini's mind was still on the cat's collar. How long was it going to take to find its meaning? It seemed like an impossible task.

"Did you guys have a good time at the library?" asked Mrs. Wellington.

"Yes, Mom, but we didn't find anything on the symbol so far."

"Why didn't you ask Kevin to come too? Maybe he could've helped."

"I don't know. I didn't want them goofing around or for us to be distracted. Besides, what if he talked too much? We can't afford anybody else founding out about this."

"I guess you're right. Just make sure you include him next time. He is feeling kind of left out."

"Yeah, I will."

"Anyone finding anything suspicious about you?"

"Yeah, there is this guy, Keith, that's getting on my case the whole time. Yesterday at the movies, he made a comment on my eyes changing or being different whatever. I hope he doesn't make it an issue."

"Houdini, you have to be so careful about this until we figure this out. You have to lie low. Anything can happen if this would to come out…"

"I know, Mom, I know."

They rode in silence the rest of the way home. His mind kept going back to the movie theater. He had to learn to control his mood, his emotions. His mom was right, but how? He didn't tell his mom because he didn't want to worry her, but it wasn't just Keith. Other people at school were getting suspicious too. At PE class, he ran too fast, he was too flexible, and he jumped too high. In regular classes, he was always too jumpy. Any little noise would startle him. And when he tried to pay attention, his eyes were too focused, too intense. At best he was really odd, and people were beginning to notice.

*****

"Have you found out any news about the cat's collar or the cat's whereabouts?" asked the elderly man to John.

"Yes, I found out about the family that I think adopted the cat. The Wellington family. I overheard some teenagers talking about it at the Humane Society. From what I heard, it sounds like our cat. I already went through the Yellow Pages trying to find an address for them. Incredibly, there is more than one Wellington family around here. We got three different addresses from the Yellow Pages. But don't worry, we will find the collar."

"Yes, once we find the collar, we will be home free," replied the man. "There are no witnesses to our practice. And the cat is not a menace, since we erased his memory. You took care of that before you dropped him off."

"Yes," he said, lost in thought, his mind going back to that night… Everything happened so fast. Someone had alerted the police about strange activities in an abandoned warehouse. That night they were trying frantically to get rid of all evidences of their practices. People were running in the dark using only flashlights, trying not to call attention to the building. The animals were acting out that night.

They felt that something wasn't right, so they were more active than ever.

They had a truck parked on the back of the warehouse. And they were busy trying to get the animals out in time.

He took the cat out of the cage and placed him on a table. Sitting on the medical table next to him were two syringes with the serum that he was supposed to administer to the cat in order to erase his memory and prevent any kind of mutation. He was injecting the cat with the first syringe when they heard the police siren in the distance. They all panicked. He could hear the voices around him in a panic.

"People, hurry, we have to get out of here. The police is on its way." People were rushing to get the animals in the truck on time to escape the police. He remembered his hand shaking as he injected the cat with the first syringe. The cat hissed and twisted in pain, knocking the second syringe off the table, which shattered into pieces when it hit the floor. There was no time for getting another syringe ready. He grabbed the cat by the back of his neck and tried to shove it in the cage. The cat kept twisting and fighting not to get in the cage. It scratched his hands, drawing blood. The police lights were showing through the windows now. He pushed the cat in a last effort to get him in it, got the cat into the crate, and closed the crate's door. Running as fast as he could, he jumped into the back of the truck, cat in hand, and closed the back door.

"Move! Go, go!" he screamed loud enough for the driver to hear it from the driver's seat. The driver floored the accelerator, and the truck disappeared through the back roads. Since they had a head start and knew the area well, they were able to escape the police. He rested his back against the wall of the truck, with his heart pounding out of his chest with fear.

He remembered the shattered syringe on the floor and panicked again. No one could find out about it. He wouldn't tell, he thought, and as long as he didn't tell, no one would be the wiser.

"John, are you okay?" asked the other man. "You look pale."

"Oh no. I'm fine," he replied, trying to hide his fear. "It's just a matter of time now before we find the collar," he said.

Chapter 9

The next day, the Wellington family went on a family outing. They were celebrating Mrs. Wellington's promotion at work. They had promoted her to manager position. She was very pleased about this. She would have to work less hours, and she would be supervising the employees instead of taking care of the customers herself. She had an office now, and she wouldn't have to stand on her feet so much. This promotion was music to her ears. She would have more time to spend with the kids. As it was, she hardly saw them. It had taken a while, but finally all her hard work had paid off.

They left the house around 5:00 p.m. It was already getting dark. It got dark a lot earlier now being winter. They were all wearing their best clothes. Mrs. Wellington had insisted on it. Kevin and Houdini were wearing a tie. They both complained about it but eventually gave up and wore it. It was the first time that Houdini had gone anywhere without his black hoodie. He felt naked, but it was a special occasion, and they both wanted to please their mom. Anna looked very pretty. She was wearing a very pretty pink dress she had bought for the father-daughter dance at school last Valentine's Day. Mrs. Wellington had made reservations at one of the most expensive restaurants in town. It would be nice to sit down and be served instead of doing the serving herself like she always did at the diner. It would make her feel special for sure.

In the car ride to the restaurant, they talked about trivial things and joked. Houdini was feeling very grateful that this was his family. How lucky was he to have found people that loved him and accepted him for who he was, even though he himself didn't know who that was. Most importantly, they had made him a part of their family. He knew he loved them all. He loved Anna, so sweet and caring. He heard about how much she had loved him as a cat and how much she cried when she lost him. There was a bond between them that would never be broken. It was fortunate that she had picked him from the Humane Society, he thought. Who knew what could have happened if she hadn't picked him? He would be forever grateful to her. And Kevin was his brother. No doubt they argued and fight sometimes like brothers do. But he couldn't think of a better brother to have. He definitely had his back, he thought. This was his family, he thought, and he knew that he would kill anyone that tried to harm them in any way. He was sure of that.

They arrived at the restaurant about 5:30, and they were walked to a table by the window. In the summertime people sat at the outside of the restaurant. The restaurant was always full. The terrace was always decorated with clear Christmas lights. There were tables and chairs outside. And in the middle of the terrace was a beautiful stone firepit with chairs all around it for people to sit by the fire. But today they had to sit inside. It was too cold outside. Through the window they could see the outside of the restaurant. It was empty. No one dared sit outside in this weather, but the fire was going and still was beautiful to look at.

Halfway through the dinner, Houdini and Kevin excused themselves to go to the restroom. They flagged down a waitress and told her that today was their mom's birthday. They knew it wasn't true. But they wanted to make the day more special for their mom. Besides, they were already laughing thinking about their mom's face when they would come to the table singing and clapping, holding a cake. It would be hilarious.

They went back and sat at the table. They had a great time, the food was great, and so was the conversation. Toward the end of the night, when it was time for dessert, they saw a big group of people approaching the table, holding a lid cake. Mrs. Wellington thought nothing about it—this happened all the time at restaurants—until they stopped at her table, clapping and singing "Happy Birthday" while they put a big hat on her head. She sat still; she was very surprised and confused. But she didn't want to interrupt the singing. Kevin and Houdini were bending over with laughter, holding on to their stomach.

On the way back home from the restaurant, they were still talking and laughing about the prank they played on their mother.

"Oh, Mom, you shoulda seen yourself. Your face was so funny," said Kevin.

"Nice one, guys. I hope you're happy. I was so embarrassed."

"At least we got free cake," said Houdini.

"That was mean, you guys," said Anna, trying hard not to laugh.

"Yeah," said Mrs. Wellington. "You guys were lucky I went along with it. I didn't want to make you guys look like liars."

They were turning the street to their house when they saw police car lights in front of their house. When they arrived, there were two police cars on the driveway. They all got out of the car and rushed over to see what was happening.

"May I help you, ma'am?" said one of the police officers to Mrs. Wellington. "This is a police matter."

"Oh, we live here," said Mrs. Wellington. "What happened?"

"We got a call about a break-in in progress from the owner. Apparently, she was sleeping when she heard noises in the house and called 911. By the time we got here, she was lying unconscious on the floor. And the house was ransacked."

"Is she okay?" asked Mrs. Wellington.

"We don't know, ma'am. She was rushed to the hospital. Are you family?"

"No, we live in the guest house on the back. Was there anything missing from the house?"

"We don't know, ma'am. We couldn't ask since she was unconscious, but all the valuable things appear to be untouched, so we are ruling a robbery out. It seemed someone was looking for something in particular, we don't know what, but it sure is a mess in there."

"Was she hurt bad?"

"We are not at liberty to discuss that with non-family members. You would have to call the hospital. Does she have any family we can contact?"

"None that I know of. Her husband passed away a few years ago, and she lives alone. Can't imagine who would want to hurt her."

"Well, here is my card," said the police officer. "If you remember something or you need to talk, give me a call."

They all walked to their house. Once they got in, Mrs. Wellington called the hospital to find out about Mrs. Anderson's health. She was happy to hear that Mrs. Anderson was okay. She had been hit on the back of the head with a heavy object, but she was going to be all right. They were keeping her in the hospital for observation overnight. But most likely she would go home the following day.

After she hung up the phone, she still couldn't believe what had just happened. Who would want to hurt an old lady? And what were they looking for? It was unreal. Things like this didn't happen there.

After the police left, Houdini and Kevin walked to the main house and looked through the windows. The place was a mess. Things were thrown all over the floor; all desk drawers were open. All the kitchen cabinet doors were open, and the drawers too. Even the bed's mattress was moved out of place. Whoever had broken into the house was definitely looking for something. But what? What can the old lady have that was so important to someone? And what if their house was next?

That night Houdini had nightmares again. He was walking. Someone was leading him, but he couldn't see his face. He only saw his back. The person was wearing a white lab coat.

The man bent down and removed a piece of carpet from the floor, exposing a door. He then pressed a button hidden in the wall, and the door opened with a loud screech. Inside was a ladder that led to the bottom floor.

When they finished going down the ladder, they found themselves in an underground lab. There were big commercial computers and lab equipment lining the walls. There were lab tubes and microscopes.

In the middle of the room stood an operating table under very big fluorescent lamps that hung from the ceiling. There was a smaller adjacent room with a large window in the middle of the wall that separated the two rooms, and in the enclosed room was a chair. The chair was a mix between a dentist chair and a doctor's bed. Lots of wires and belts were connected from it to a big machine next to it. Across the chair on the opposite wall was what looked like a big-screen TV or computer monitor, he wasn't sure. He had been there before many times, he had no doubt. His heart began to pound, his palms were getting sweaty, and then he woke up, sweating and panting again. *Another nightmare,* he thought, trying to regulate his breathing.

Nightmares were very common to him, but they were getting more real all the time. Maybe he was beginning to remember. Maybe his memory was coming back.

The next morning, he was very tired again when the alarm went off. Every time he had a nightmare, he was drained the following day. But he made an effort and got ready for school. He was worried about what would be waiting for him at school. He was dreading math class.

He didn't want to have another confrontation with Keith. But he knew that after the incident at the movie theater, Keith wasn't going to let it go that easy. Keith had seen his eyes change. He was on to him. He knew how bullies worked. All bullies have low self-esteem and put other people down to make themselves feel better. They prey on the weak, and now he had something on him. Something he was trying to hide.

Keith had the upper hand. He would have to deny it if Keith decided to say anything about his eyes. And he would try very hard to stay calm. He couldn't afford to lose control in front of everyone. Or his secret would be out.

On the other hand, he was happy to see Krissy again. They had texted a couple of times over the weekend, but he couldn't wait to see her again.

He kept daydreaming about her. And it was hard to keep her off his mind. She was beautiful; everyone could see that, but it wasn't just her looks he liked. She was sweet and funny, and he loved how overprotective she was of him, he thought with a smile.

School went on without any major problems. He was happy to see when he got to math class that Keith was absent that day, so he would not have to worry about him at least until tomorrow. Jake had met him up at school in the morning before class started to let him know he had been looking for the symbol on his own time and had found something similar to it. But he needed Houdini to look at it. They decided on meeting sometime during the week in the library and work on it.

At lunchtime Houdini looked for Krissy. He spotted her from a distance. It looked to him like she was doing the same thing. When their eyes met, she looked away, embarrassed. He walked toward her, trying very hard not to look too happy about it. They sat together for lunch, they talked about the previous weekend, and they even held hands under the table.

On the way home from school, Kevin and he were talking about the break-in in the main house. They could not get it out of their minds.

"What do you think the people that broke in the house were looking for?" asked Kevin.

"I don't know, but it got to be something really important for them to hit Mrs. Anderson unconscious."

"I guess, they didn't want to be recognized. She probably caught them in the act," said Kevin.

"Yeah, they could've killed her too, so I don't think this is the kind of people you want to mess with," said Houdini.

"Do you think they will be back for whatever they're looking for?"

"I don't know, but if they do, it would be risky. The police is going to be patrolling the area at least for a couple of nights. They're still investigating what happened."

"It's scary though. Our house is right behind hers. I wonder if this was an isolated case or if they would be trying to break into our house next. We share the same address. And we weren't there last night. The lights were off in our house. Maybe they didn't realize that there were people living in our house," said Kevin.

"Yeah, you're right. I hope we are overthinking this. But we better be alert, keep our eyes open. You never know."

The bus came to a stop, and they got out and waited for Anna's bus before they started walking together toward their house. Houdini was very aware of the neighborhood dogs now. He tried to walk as far away from them as possible and he was always ready to take off running if needed. As they were approaching the house, they were surprised to see a black car driving very slowly down the road. That was very strange, they thought. There was hardly any traffic going by their house on a regular basis. The only traffic was from neighbors, and they didn't have many. Only a handful of houses were in that area.

They knew all their neighbors, and this wasn't a car they recognized.

As the car drove by them, they tried to look at the driver, but the car's windows had a dark tint on them, and you could not see inside the car.

Maybe it was an undercover police car, they thought, but they were going to mention it to their mom just in case.

Chapter 10

John was meeting with his boss again. He was worried about what the outcome of the meeting would be. He was hoping to have better news to deliver, he thought as he walked into the room.

They tried to meet in different places all the time so as not to raise any suspicion. This time they were meeting in a coffee shop in town. They both ordered a regular coffee and sat on the far back of the coffee shop away from people. They didn't want their conversation to be overheard.

"How's it going? Any news about the matter?" asked the old man.

"Well, I don't have as good of a news as I thought I would have by now."

"What do you mean?"

"The break-in did not go as planned. This is the third house we checked. And we have found nothing so far. The only thing we got was the police interested in why there are so many break-ins in the area. We are really hoping they don't put two and two together and realize that all the houses' owners have the same last name."

"What happened to this last one?"

"Well, we didn't find the collar, and no signs of the cat either. It's like the cat has vanished into thin air. We still can't figure it out."

"Did you break into the house?"

"We did. We were in the middle of looking for the collar or the cat when the old lady walked into the room. It was dark, so I don't think she saw our faces. But she was freaking out. So we had no choice but to hit her over the head to keep her from screaming. She managed to call the police before we knew about her being there. We had no choice but to take off running. When we heard the police sirens, we hid behind some bushes on the back of the house until they left, and we then called for someone to pick us up. Good we didn't drive there, or we would not have time to get away. They would've found the car for sure and traced back to us. By the way, when we were hiding, we noticed a smaller house on the back of the main house, kind of a guest house, I guess. We did not see anybody there. But I guess we have to go back and check that one too. You never know."

"Hitting the lady was not part of the plan. No one was supposed to get hurt."

"I know, boss, but we had no choice."

"You guys are a bunch of incompetents," he said through clenched teeth. Trying very hard not to raise his voice, he said, "You were not supposed to get the police involved. We are trying to stay away from the police, remember? Not call their attention."

"I know, I know. We are going to take it easy for a while now until the heat dies off. I'm going to have to go back to volunteering at the shelter. And try to find out the address of the family that actually adopted the cat to make sure we have the right house this time, before we attempt anything else."

"Must I remind you again that we are running out of time? I was informed they have seem the police going through the warehouse a couple of times. I'm sure they are still investigating. We need to get our hands on that collar."

"I know, boss, I know. Trust me, I'm on it.

That night over supper, the conversation turned into the break-in the night before. Mrs. Anderson was not back yet. Mrs. Wellington had called the hospital inquiring about her and was told that they had decided to keep her in the hospital an extra day as a precaution. They were worried about her being elderly and alone in the house so soon after the accident. Since she had no one to take care of her, they thought that in was in her best interest to keep her in the hospital. Most likely she would be going home tomorrow after the doctor saw her, she was told.

Kevin told his mom about the car they had seen early that day on the way back from school and their worrying about their house being the next target. Mrs. Wellington mentioned that she overheard some people talking at the diner about two other houses being broken into recently in the area. It seemed that that was all people were talking about. Usually there wasn't any crime happening in their small town. So news travel fast.

"Do you think this would have anything to do with me?" asked Houdini.

"I don't think so. Why would you think that?" asked Mrs. Wellington.

"I don't know, Mom. I have a feeling, I guess… we don't know anything about me. Maybe someone is after me. Look, you just said it. Nothing ever happened here before, and now all this. It makes you wonder."

"If someone would be after you, they would be looking for a cat, not a person. No one besides us knows who you are."

"I know, but I don't know for how much longer. I'm having a hard time controlling the changes. I almost changed into a cat at the movies. I can't control it, Mom."

"We will think of a way, Houdini. We are in this together. No one would find out about you. We won't let it happen, okay?"

Houdini nodded in agreement, but he was not so sure. He wished that he was as optimistic as she was.

After dinner they all sat down to watch a movie in the family room, a scary movie that Anna had suggested. They popped some popcorn and grabbed blankets to cover themselves with. Even though the heater was on, it was still cold inside the house. It was a movie about a werewolf, some old movie from the '80s teen wolf. Anna picked it because it was scary but not too scary, she said. The movie was about a boy that learned he was a werewolf. The main character, a werewolf, would change into a wolf every time there was a full moon. Eventually, people found out about him being a werewolf, and he became the most popular guy in school and so on.

Houdini wished it was that easy in real life. It was easy for the werewolf, Houdini thought to himself. The werewolf knew exactly when the change would happen, every time there was a full moon, so he could avoid it, stay home. It wasn't that easy for him though. He didn't know what caused him to change. Besides, he didn't think people would be so accepting of him in real life if they would find out about him being a cat. It was hard enough for him at school just being a little odd.

The next day at school, he had a hard time paying attention in class. All he could think about was math class. For sure Keith would be there today. When he finally got to math class, he saw Keith sitting on his usual seat in the back of the classroom. He hurried up and sat at his desk, trying not to make eye contact. He didn't want any problems. Toward the middle of the class, Houdini was feeling a little more relaxed, when the guy sitting behind him tapped him on the shoulder. When he looked back, he passed him a note and pointed at Keith. He turned around and hid the note under his notebook. He didn't want to open it yet. He wasn't ready for it. And besides, he didn't want the teacher to confiscate it.

When the bell rang, he was getting out of his chair when Keith passed by his chair and bumped into it, staring at him with a smirk on his face, and kept walking slowly toward the door, staring him down, trying to intimidate him. Houdini kept his head up and his eyes on him too. He was not going to back down. Eventually, Keith looked away and walked out the classroom door. Houdini took out the note from under his notebook and read it. In big red letters it read, "I'm on to you, freak. You're not fooling me. I will find you out."

At lunchtime, instead of going to the cafeteria to meet Krissy, he went straight to the library to meet with Jake. He really wanted to see Krissy, but he would call her later. Keith was on to him. He said it himself. And he had a feeling someone other than Keith was after him too. Finding out the meaning of the sign was way more important now. Everything else could wait. He wanted to know what Jake had found out about it. When he got to the library, Jake was already there. He went straight to the table and sat down, putting his book bag on the floor next to him. The collar was inside. He was not going to show it to Jake; he knew better. But he was going to use it as reference.

"Hey, Jake, was up?" asked Houdini, sitting next to him at the table.

"Hi, bro, I brought the book I told you about. It belongs to my dad. I found it by accident going through his medical books he keeps from when he went to school. I keep the drawing from the other day at the library, the one you made, and I think this one looks similar to it. You tell me," he said, taking the drawing out of his pocket and placing it on the table, then he opened the book to the page and put it next to the symbol on the book.

Houdini's eyes got big. He was looking down at the book, and there in front of his eyes was the symbol or part of it. The page showed a circle with a design around it in two different colors, blue and teal. The circle was made of many small circles. The lines were interchanged, making the design of the small circles. In the middle of each circle were three lines, which alternate color also. In one circle the lines would be one teal color and two green color. The next circle would have one green line and two teal color lines. This went all around the circle. In the center of the main circle was what looked like a spiral in the color gray. He remembered the symbol in the collar. It was very similar. Under the symbol, the description read "DNA chain in 3-D" (three dimension).

"Is that the symbol we have been looking for?" asked Jake. "Did we find it?"

"Kind of, I guess…" he said, looking at the sign from different angles. "The center of the symbol looks different."

"The one I saw had something different in the center. It was kind of hard to see, but I know it wasn't this."

"What do you think it means?" asked Houdini.

"I don't know. I still haven't figured it out."

"But at least we got part of it. It's a DNA chain symbol."

"Yeah… thanks, bro. You're the best. I owed you one. Got to get back to class though. Catch you later."

He was rushing down the hall; he didn't want to be late to his next class. He was looking down as he walked, when he ran into Keith, who was going into the library. *Weird,* he thought, running to class.

In class he kept thinking about the symbol. Why would a DNA strand symbol be on the cat's collar? It kind of made sense, he thought. Someone had altered the cat's DNA. Why else would a cat become human, or vice versa? He pushed the thought out of his mind. He needed to pay attention in class; there was going to be a test at the end of the week. This was the week before Thanksgiving break. He would have plenty of time to investigate next week when school was out.

After class he looked for Krissy to walk her to her bus. His face lit up with happiness when he saw her.

"Hey, I didn't see you at lunch. Are you okay?"

"Yes, sorry, I had to go to the library today, had to catch up on some schoolwork. Why? Did you miss me?" he asked with a smile on his face.

"Maybe…" she said, moving a strand of hair from her face.

"Here, let me help you," said Houdini, getting the books from her. He walked her to her bus, and right before she was getting on the bus, she turned around kissed him on the cheek and got on the bus without giving him a chance to say anything.

Houdini touched his face and smiled. Then he ran to his bus. The school bus was already in motion. Kevin saw him running after it and told the bus driver to stop. Houdini jumped in, relieved that he was not left behind.

Chapter 11

During the Thanksgiving break week, Kevin and Houdini worked on helping Houdini on developing ways to control Houdini's changes. They tried getting Houdini scared; they tried running as fast as they could. Nothing worked.

It was snowing that week. They were still worrying about the break-in next door. But nothing else had happened except on one of the nights, they woke up to some noises in the backyard. They woke up, turned all the lights, and checked all the windows and door. Everything looked secure, so they went back to bed. Maybe it was the house settling, they thought.

The next morning they found footprints on the fresh fallen snow leading to the woods behind their house. Apparently, someone was walking around the house, trying to find a way in.

Mrs. Wellington went to her purse and took out the business card that the police investigator had given her and called the number.

"Detective Harrison? Hi, this is Mrs. Wellington at 1400 Lane Brooks. We spoke the other day about a break-in at the house next door. You gave me your card."

"Oh yes, of course, how can I help you?"

"Last night we heard noises outside our house, and this morning we found footprints in the snow leading to the woods behind the house. The footprints don't match to any of our kids'. They seem to be a man's footprint."

"Was anything disturbed around the house? Any attempt to force entry?"

"No, none that I can see. We checked the windows and doors, and everything seems to be okay."

"Well, in that case, there is not much we can do. We have police patrolling the area already. I will make sure to inform them so they can keep an extra eye on the house. If anything else happens, make sure to call me immediately. You have my number."

"Yes, I will, thanks for your time."

Mrs. Wellington couldn't help but worry about it. For as long as they have lived in the house, nothing like this ever happened, and now first Mrs. Anderson next door and now this.

A couple of days before thanksgiving, Kevin and Anna left to spend Thanksgiving with their dad. Houdini stayed behind. The father didn't know about Houdini's existence. They had to keep it a secret from him. How would they explain the extra kid in the house? He would have questions that they were not able to answer.

This year it was going to be just Mrs. Wellington and Houdini for Thanksgiving dinner. But Houdini asked Jake to join them. There was only Jake and his dad in Jake's family. Jake's mom had passed away a couple of years ago. Thanksgiving was never a good time of the year for them; it brought out too many memories. It was painful still to celebrate without her. And his dad avoided celebrating it.

That day Mrs. Wellington cooked the turkey and all the trimmings. She decorated the house with pumpkins and fall foliage. The table was set with their best dishes and candles. The ambience was very festive. Even though they wished for Kevin and Anna to be with them, Mrs. Wellington was thankful that she had company. If she didn't have Houdini, she would've been alone for the holiday. They sat down at the dinner table around 7:00 p.m. Mrs. Wellington liked to have Thanksgiving dinner at night. Everything looked more festive at night, and she liked to have a candlelit dinner. She had many reasons to be thankful for this year. They were all healthy, she had gotten a promotion at work, and most importantly, she was thankful for having Houdini in her life. She had grown to love him like one of her own kids, even though she worried daily about him being found out or someone taking him away from them. She could not imagine her life without him.

After Thanksgiving dinner, Jake and Houdini went down to the basement to play Xbox. They had expended a couple of hours playing *Assassin* when Mrs. Wellington called them up to the kitchen to have pumpkin pie and hot cocoa with marshmallows and cinnamon like she liked to make it.

"Are you guys going to stay put for a while?" asked Mrs. Wellington. "I think I'm going to bed. I'm a little tired. Make sure you clean after yourself, and don't stay up too late."

"We will," said Houdini. "Good night, Mom."

Jake was sleeping over that night. They stayed up until late, talking and watching TV. They went to bed late and fell asleep quick.

Around 2:00 a.m. they woke up to a loud noise. Houdini jumped from the bed and grabbed the bat he kept next to his bed, the same one that Kevin had tried to hit him with the first night he came back. He woke up Jake, who was sleeping on Kevin's bed.

"Jake! Wake up, bro. I heard a noise. Let's go check it out."

Jake jumped out of bed, half asleep. "What?"

"I think there is someone in the house. Come with me," he said, whispering.

They went down the stairs, trying hard not to make noises. Once they got to the family room, they saw the door to the entertainment center was open, and so were the drawers. Houdini's heart started to pound hard. Jake looked at Houdini with big open eyes as they walked toward the kitchen. When they turned the corner to the kitchen, they saw the silhouette of two men in the dark. They were wearing black clothes and a black ski mask over their faces. Houdini's blood felt icy cold in his veins. He was shaking with fear. He looked at Jake, and Jake looked scared too. Houdini gestured at Jake to turn on the lights. At the same time Houdini screamed at the top of his lungs, "I have a gun, and I know how to use it!" The two men took off running out of the kitchen door.

Houdini and Jake took off running after them. They were afraid. Adrenaline was pumping through their bodies, but Houdini wasn't going to let them get away this time. He needed to find out who they were and what they wanted. He was tired of being afraid. The men kept running through the woods, and so did Houdini and Jake after them. They got to a clearing in the woods. They could not see the two men anymore. Everything was dark and quiet. Houdini's heart was pounding out of his chest; his body was shaking with fear. They were walking slowly, trying to find where the men were hiding, when from one of the bushes jumped one of the men holding a flashlight to Houdini's face, while the other took a hold of Jake. Houdini jumped back with fear.

Jake and the two men stood in shock. Right in front of them was not a kid but a cat.

"John, that's our cat!" screamed the second man, pointing the flashlight in the direction where Houdini had disappeared running. They both took off running after Houdini, forgetting all about Jake, who was in shock and too afraid to even move.

Houdini kept running as fast as his legs could carry him, the two men right on his tail. He was way too fast for them. This time he was very aware that he was a cat. He felt agile, fast, and light. H felt the wind on his fur, and he could see as well as daytime. He kept zigzagging through the trees, trying to lose the men that were following him. Before he knew it, he was in front of a pond. It was a big pond, he could see it. Clearly there was no other place to run, no tree to climb, just water in front of him. He turned his body around. His back was arched, and his fur was up. His ears were pushed back on his head. He was hissing at the approaching men, getting ready to defend himself.

"Get the cat! Get the cat!" he heard the man said. "We can't let him get away."

The man kept walking slowly toward him, one on each side, trying to block his way out. The flashlight was pointed at his face, making it very hard for Houdini to see. He saw the light approaching. He had to act on instinct. His heart was pounding fast. He had to do it. He just jumped toward the light, grabbing on to one of the guy's shirt and scratching his face with his free paw. The guy screamed in pain, holding his face and pushing him toward the floor, trying to get him off him. Houdini landed on his paws. The second man launched at Houdini, trying to grab him. Houdini twisted his body, getting loose from his hold, and ran between the man's legs, making him lose his balance and fall face-first on the ground.

Houdini took off running back toward the woods. He ran as fast as he could without looking back. He hid in some bushes and waited a long time. After a while he didn't hear voices anymore or footsteps. His heartbeat was slowly coming down and then blackness.

When he made it back to the house, there were police cars all around the house. From where he was, he could see Jake sitting on the sofa and her mom talking to a police officer at the front door. He decided it would be best to wait for the police to leave before he went back home. He waited behind the house awhile. When he saw the police leave, then he entered the house through the kitchen door.

His mom ran toward him and hugged him the minute she saw him.

"Oh my god, honey, are you all right?" she said, checking him all over. "I was worried sick about you."

"I'm fine, Mom. Really, I'm okay."

Houdini looked over her shoulder to see Jake, who was staring at him as if he was seeing a ghost. His eyes opened wide in disbelief.

"Mom, did you explain to him everything?"

"Yes, I did. But still it's going to take a while. You know how it is."

Houdini walked over to the sofa and sat next to Jake, who moved a little away from him.

"Hey, bro, are you okay? Are we good?"

Jake nodded. "Why didn't you tell me?"

"It's not something you tell everybody. I still don't understand it myself, and besides, you would not have believed even if I told you. You saw it, and you're still having trouble believing it."

"Yes, I guess you're right. Is this the reason you were so determined to find the meaning of the symbol?"

"Yes, that symbol is the only clue I have about who I am or where I came from. It was on the cat's collar when they found me."

"Do you have it with you?"

"Yes, I do, it's in a safe place. I will show it to you, but now is not the time. It's late, I'm tired. We better go back to bed. Can I count on you to keep the secret?"

"Yes, bro, you have my word. I know what it is like to be different. We'll figure it out."

Houdini was so tired he passed out the minute his head hit the pillow.

Chapter 12

The next morning over breakfast, they discussed the details about the previous night.

Mrs. Wellington told them that she had woken up the night before by all the commotion. She was scared and confused she didn't know what was happening. She knew that Houdini and Jake were not home, so she waited for at least one of them to be back before calling the police. When Jake got back and told her what had happened, she tried to calm him down. She could hardly make out what he was saying. She sat him down and told him the whole story, all they knew about Houdini. She made him swear he would keep the secret, and only then did she call the police to report the break-in. The police had gotten there in minutes. She had not mentioned Houdini being missing. She did not want to bring attention to Houdini. She just said someone had broken in the house. The police asked if there was anything missing from the house. She said she did not think so. And they took time dusting for fingerprints. The footprints outside of the house were too messy to be identified. They looked like they were trampled on, but the police found a footprint on the side of the house under one of the windows. This print was intact. They made a cast of it to take to headquarters for investigation.

"Mom, I was right," said Houdini. "I told you they were after me. I had a feeling this had something to do with me."

"How do you know it's you they were after? Nothing was missing."

"I think they were after the cat's collar originally, but now they'll be after me."

"After you? Why? What do you mean?"

"Yesterday when I changed into a cat, I heard one of the man tell the other one, 'That's our cat. Don't let him get away.' And they went after me. It took everything I had to get away from them. I know they will be back. They know who I am, they saw my face, and they know where I live."

Mrs. Wellington stayed silent for a while, trying to assimilate what she was hearing. Her biggest nightmare was coming true; they were after Houdini. She had to fight back the tears that were welling in her eyes.

"Well, the police is after them, honey. Maybe the police will find them before they find you. We just have to be extra careful now, that's all."

"Yeah, you're right…"

John was on his car on the way to meeting his boss. He had not slept all night, worrying and thinking about how he would break the news to his boss. The collar was nowhere to be found. And the cat they were after was no longer a cat but a kid. And it was all his fault, he knew it.

If only he had administered the second shot to the cat that night at the lab, this would not have had happened. The shot was supposed to stop the gene mutation, to stop all this from happening. But he had failed to inject the cat with it. He was responsible for the mutation, and he had lied about it too. Things were getting way out of control, and it was all his fault. He moved the car's rearview mirror to look at his face. On the left side of his face, right underneath his left eye, were four deep bloody lines that went down his check to the side of his mouth. He touched his swollen cheek, exhaling a deep breath. He moved the mirror back to its original position. He kept thinking about last night. For all the time they had the cat, the cat had never mutated. He was sure of it. They would not have gotten rid of the cat if they had foreseen anything like this happening. The shot was just a prevention. They never thought this would actually happen. He was dreading what his boss's reaction was going to be when he found out about the whole thing. The break-in last night had been a total fiasco. The police was now closer than ever to finding out who they were. And now the kid. He wondered how much the kid knew, how much he remembered.

There are getting to be too many witnesses, he thought. H only knew one thing: they had to get the cat back. And it had to be soon, very soon.

The rest of the Thanksgiving break went by fast. Houdini kept looking over his shoulder wherever he went. He met Jake at the library one of the days and took the collar to show it to him just like he promised. The only reason why they met at the library was because they needed a safe place to meet away from the house. He didn't know if the house was being watched. Jake brought some more of his dad's medical books for them to go through it and try to find the meaning to the rest of the collar's symbol.

Houdini took the cat's collar out of his pocket and handed it to Jake, looking both ways, making sure that he was not followed there.

"Okay, here it is! This is the collar they are after. The big enigma."

"Wow, that's pretty cool. What is it a made of?"

"I don't know. It seems to be some kind of metal. But I've never seen any metal like this before."

Jake turned the collar around in his hand, trying to examine every inch of it.

"Is this what you were talking about?" said Jake, pointing to the center of the medallion.

"Yes, that's it."

"It's very small. We are going to have to find a magnifying glass. See if the librarian has one we can borrow?"

Jake opened some of the books on the table and began looking through the pages carefully.

A little while later, Houdini came back holding a magnifying glass and handed it over to Jake. "Any luck?"

"Nope, let's see," he said, holding the magnifying glass right on the medallion. They both tried very hard to see through it at the same time, bumping their heads.

"Hey, watch it, bro," said Jake, massaging his forehead.

"I think it's… a bean?" said Houdini, closing one eye, trying to focus.

"A bean? Why would it be a bean?"

"I don't know. It looks like a lima bean or a capital letter *B*, I guess. It looks like there is a crescent moon or something in the upper part."

"Wait, let me see," said Jake, taking the magnifying glass from Houdini.

"Yes, I think you are right. That's what it looks like. What else is on it?"

Right on the reverse of the collar reads "Adam" and the number 2008

"The number? Or the year? What do you think?"

"I don't know. I had expended hours looking at it, days trying to figure it out, and still it makes no sense to me."

"Well, let's look through the books and see if we find something like it."

"Maybe we'll get lucky again."

They spent hours going through book after book. They were about to give up for the day, when they came across something similar in one of the pages.

"Hey, bro, check this out!" exclaimed Jake. "Where is the collar? Give it to me."

Houdini handed over the collar to Jake, and Jake places it right next to the drawing of the sign on the page.

"Dude, I think this may be it! Look! It's almost the same," he said, pointing at the sign.

"What is it though?"

Jake pointed at the bottom of the picture. It read, "Letter B Embrion baby reproduction, birth symbol blue."

They both looked at each other.

"It's a symbol for a baby boy embryo inside a DNA chain. It is… me." Houdini kept looking at the book's page and back at the collar in disbelief. Yes, there it was. No doubt what looked like a bean was a fetus, and what they thought was a crescent moon was not a moon, but an eye. There was a line that looked like a smile, making the shape of the mouth. It was a baby Embrion symbol.

Jake's dad picked them up from the library this time and drove them home. Mrs. Wellington had to stay home to wait for Kevin and Anna, who were coming back from their dad's house. On the way home, Jake's dad kept making small talk in the car. Houdini was half listening to it. His mind was somewhere else.

"So how did it go?" asked Jake's dad. "You guys learn anything new today?"

"Yes, I guess. We were working on a project for science class," Jake lied.

"Yeah? How's it going?"

"It's doing good. We made some progress."

"Jake, I saw you took my old school books. I'm glad to see you're taking an interest in medicine and science. You know what they say, the apple does not fall far from the tree. Maybe you end up following my footsteps."

"Yeah, who knows?" said Jake, trying to change the conversation.

Houdini was quiet, staring out of the car's window, his mind lost in thoughts. They had found the meaning of the symbol. But it meant nothing to him. He was as confused as ever.

They arrived at the house. He thanked Jake's dad for the ride home and said bye to Jake.

He went into the house in a hurry. He was looking forward to seeing Kevin and Anna back home again; he really missed them.

Houdini told them everything that happened in their absence, the break-in in the house, how he had changed into a cat in front of Jake, the two men that were pursuing them, how the police was investigating the case, etc.

He also told them about what Jake and he had found out about the meaning of the symbol. They all agreed that they had to be way more alert now. They had to have their eyes wide-open. Anything could happen now, at any minute.

Houdini had been texting Krissy on and off all during Thanksgiving break. He had not mentioned anything to her about the break-in in the house or what had happened with Jake. There were too many people that knew about him already, including people he didn't want for them to know. Krissy would not understand. And besides, he would not want her to look at him any different. He didn't want her to see him as a freak. So far, besides his family and Jake, she was the one good thing that was working in his life. He knew she liked him; he could see it in her eyes every time she looked at him. He could not believe it at times. She was one of the most beautiful girls in school, the most beautiful in his opinion. And he was fortunate enough that she liked him—him out of all people, he thought. He was going to ask her out again. He could not wait until school was back to see her again.

Chapter 13

It was really cold now to do anything outdoor, so the places they could go were limited. Maybe ice skating. There was an ice skating rink in town, or bowling could be an option too. Maybe her mom could drop her off there, and they could meet as a group. Wherever he went had to be a place with a lot of people around. He did not want to be where he would be an easy prey. Those men were after him.

He talked over with Kevin and Jake, and they decided that ice skating would be the most fun. He called Krissy and asked her out to the skating rink. She said she'd be there, with Stacey of course. They agreed to meet on Friday, around 7:00 p.m.

On Friday Houdini asked Mrs. Wellington to drive them to the skating rink. She agreed to drop them off on the way to work. But they would have to wait there until she was out of work to pick them up. The skating rink was in town, but not in the best part of town. It was kind of secluded. It was surrounded by warehouses and outlet stores that were not open at night, but the place was well lit up and was always full of people, so Houdini felt safe going there. On the way over there, Mrs. Wellington was talking on the phone with Anna, giving her instructions about not opening the door to anyone and to call her if she heard or saw anything suspicious. Anna didn't want to stay alone in the house, so she had a friend over to keep her company.

"If you guys get hungry, there is pizza in the refrigerator, just put it in the microwave for a couple of minutes and it should be fine. And don't stay up to late, okay? We will be home soon." She was in the middle of the conversation when she took a wrong turn, going a different way than she usually went. They had gone a couple of blocks in the wrong direction when she noticed.

"Anna, honey, I have to let you go. I have to turn around. Listen, don't forget to call me if anything happens. I'll have the phone right next to me, okay?"

Mrs. Wellington hung up the phone and got into a driveway to turn the car around. When the headlight shone on the building, Houdini's heart skipped a beat. This place was very familiar to him. He had seen this building before, he was sure of it. He wasn't sure if he was remembering it or if he had seen it in his nightmare. But he was almost sure that he could describe the inside of it without even going inside. This got to be the place he came from, he thought. It seemed to be abandoned. He tried very hard to memorize the address; "1252 Old Mill Way," he repeated a couple of times in his head. He didn't want to worry his mom, and he wasn't sure if they were going to believe him. So he kept it to himself.

He had to come back here again. So he concentrated on learning the way. *Left then right, one traffic light, and then right again. Got it!* He thought to himself.

Mrs. Wellington dropped them off in front of the skating rink and drove away, letting them know that she would be back for them in a few hours and asking them to stay safe and out of trouble.

"Guys, did you see that building where we stopped to turn around?"

"Yeah, what about it?" asked Kevin.

"I think that's where they used to keep me. I'm almost sure of it."

"How do you know, bro?" asked Jake.

"I've seen that place before in my dreams. I recognized the building. I didn't want to say anything because I didn't want to worry Mom, but I have to go back there. I need to go inside, see if that's really the place. Are you guys up for it?"

"When, now? How about the girls."

"No, not now. The girls can't know anything about this. This has to stay between us. We will go in the skating rink, hung with the girls, and when they go home, we'll walk to the place. Mom won't be here until late. Fridays are always busy at the diner. We'll make it back before she gets here. She'll never know. What you guys say?"

"Sure, we're in. Let's do it," said Jake.

They all walked into the skating rink. The place was really full. They walked over to the desk, paid for it, got their skates, and sat down on a bench to put them on. Houdini got his cell phone out and called Krissy's number.

The lights were low, and the music was loud. Krissy's phone was ringing when he spotted her on the floor, already skating next to Stacey. He hung up the phone and went to meet her.

He was having a hard time keeping his balance with the skate on. His legs were shaking, and his ankles kept twisting. He guessed skating was not something he had done before. He had to hold on to the wall in order to walk. He entered the ice skating rink very slowly, holding on to the wall. His feet kept slipping; he had to move slow, looking down to retain his balance and not fall onto the ice. He looked up trying to see if Krissy had seen him. But to his relief, she didn't seem to know that he was there. He decided to go at list once around the rink before letting her know he was here. He didn't want her to see him skating so goofy. Whose idea was it to go ice skating? Oh yeah, it was his idea. Bad move, he thought to himself, holding tight to the glass wall. He kept his distance from Krissy and Stacey. He tried going a little faster then letting go of the wall. He was doing a little better when Kevin and Jake came skating fast toward him, braking right next to him, splashing him with ice.

"Dude, what's up? Never ice skated before? Let's go," said Kevin, showing off, turning around and skating backward.

Jake passed him too, laughing. Houdini kept skating carefully. He wasn't about to fall down. He hated getting wet.

He went a couple of times around trying to get the hang of it, making sure that he was not seen by Krissy. Finally he was feeling a little more confident, so he called to Krissy on the other side of the rink, skating toward her. Krissy stopped and waited for him. He was halfway across the ice when two little kids cut in front of him. He tried hard to avoid them but lost his balance. He twisted his body a couple of times, trying to regain his balance, but ended up falling backward right on the ice. He was embarrassed; he felt his face getting hot. He tried to get up but kept losing his balance and falling. Krissy could not contain her laughter. It took her a while to stop laughing before she skated toward him to help him get up.

"Hey, you okay?" she said, giving Houdini a hand.

"Yeah, I'm fine," said Houdini, standing up and brushing the ice off his jeans, which were really wet.

"Let's go meet the rest of the group."

They were skating slowly, when they heard the announcer say through the microphone, "This song goes to all the couples out there."

People started to get out of the skating rink, and only couples remained. The lights went low, and the song started to play.

Houdini was kind of glad that it was a slow song. It would be easier to skate to it. He held Krissy's hand, and they skated together. Krissy turned around and skated backward a couple of times. But he would not dare do it; he didn't want to fall again and make a fool of himself.

After the slow song was over, they got out of the rink and met the others at the cafeteria.

When the waitress showed up to their table to take their order, they could not agree on what pizza they wanted. Houdini wanted anchovies on the pizza. Everyone else thought it was gross.

"What? Anchovies?" said the girls in unison. "Who eats that?"

Kevin and Jake looked at Houdini and then at each other.

"Hey, it's okay," said Jake. "We can get anchovies on half the pizza. That way everyone is happy," he said, winking at Houdini.

They ordered the pizza and hot cocoa; it was too cold for sodas.

They all talked for a while and laughed, mostly about Houdini's fall.

Chapter 14

After the girls left, the guys got out of the building, closed the zippers on their jackets, put their hoods up, and took off on the direction of the warehouse. I was really cold and dark. The temperature must've been in the thirties, and the wind was strong. Almost immediately they regretted leaving the skating rink. But Houdini was determined to find this place. They walked a little and ran a little, trying to stay warm. The streets were deserted at this time at night, especially in this industrial area. But there was a full moon out, and they could see perfectly well even though it wasn't dark. The dark never bothered Houdini; he could see perfectly well in the dark anyway.

He kept repeating the directions on reverse. Left on the first traffic light, two blocks after left again, and then right. Finally they were in front of the building, 1252 Old Mill Way.

They were all out of breath from running. They took the time to catch their breaths back before walking around the building.

The windows to the building were boarded up, so they could not see inside.

"Are you sure this is the place?" asked Jake.

"Yes, I'm positive. I can feel it. Let's go around the back. I'm sure there's got to be a way in somewhere."

They walked toward the back of the building, looking over their shoulders, making sure not to be seen.

Everything was closed, all windows and doors; there was no way in. They were getting despair when they spotted a small round glass window on the back side of the building.

"Look, there is a window up there," said Kevin, pointing up.

"Yeah, I see it. But how are we going to reach it?"

"Let's look around. Maybe we can find something we can use to climb, maybe a ladder or a box, I don't know. Something."

They all walked around the building and the woods behind it, looking for something to use. There was an old bucket and some wooden boxes, but they had been left out in the outside weather too long, and they were rotting. They could not hold their weight.

Houdini had an idea. "Let's get on each other's shoulders. Once I get in, I will open the side door from the inside and let you guys in."

"Cool, let's do it!" said Kevin.

"How are we going to do this? Let's think."

"Jake, you are the tallest and heaviest, so you should go on the bottom, then Kevin then me."

"Okay," said Jake, kneeling down so Kevin could sit on his shoulders. He stood up kind of shaky, trying to keep his balance and not drop Kevin.

They were both leaning against the wall under the window. They could almost reach it but not quite.

"Let go, bro. He is heavy. Get to it," said Jake.

Houdini took out his boots. "Okay, how are we going to do this?"

"Hold on to my hand," said Kevin, reaching down to him.

Kevin was pulling him up, and Houdini was climbing on Jake's side between Jake and the wall. It was hard to hold on to. Finally he got to hold on to Kevin's shoulders and climbed on it.

He finally reached the window, but when he pushed on it, the window was closed.

"Dude, the window is closed," said Houdini, looking down at the ground, trying to find something they could use to break the glass.

"Look, there is a rock next to you, grab it."

Jake bent his knees very carefully to grab the rock. The boys were too heavy he almost lost balance and fell, but he got the rock and stood up slowly. He passed the rock up to Kevin, and Kevin passed it up to Houdini.

Houdini broke the glass of the window, making sure to knock down every piece of glass. He did not want to get cut.

"Hurry," cried Jake. "It's getting too heavy. My legs are shaking."

Houdini got a hold of the side of the window and got in halfway, one leg in, one leg out. Jake got Kevin off his shoulders.

Houdini took out his cell phone and turned on the flashlight to see inside. Apparently, it was the bathroom. Right under the window, he could see the sink. Very carefully he maneuvered himself around and put a foot on top of the sink, holding on to the window, and then got down.

"I'm in!" he yelled for the guys to hear. Pointing the flashlight in front of himself, he walked carefully toward the side door and opened it.

"Come in quick. Don't let anybody see you," said Houdini, looking both ways.

Kevin and Jake entered the building and turned on their cell phone's flashlight.

The inside of the building was pitch-black. The only lights were the light of their cell phones' flashlights. They looked around. There were empty animal cages left on the floor, but other than that, it looked pretty bare.

"Dude, there is nothing here. This can't be the place."

"It is," said Houdini, his heartbeat raising. "It was here, I remember well. Just follow me. I know where I'm going."

He walked toward the back of the warehouse. "It was here, I'm sure of it. There was a carpet here," he said, kneeling down on the floor and feeling the surface of the wood for any indentation. "The wall! It was in the wall." He stood up and turned to the wall, touching its surface.

The wall looked like an ordinary pine wood plank wall. He kept going over the eyes on the wood. None gave in. "I was here. I remember." He pressed one of the eyes close to the corner of the wall, and a door on the floor opened with a loud screech. They all turned around to look at it.

"I knew it! Let's go." They pointed the flashlight at the hole in the floor. It was dark, but they could see a ladder going down.

"I'm going down. Who's with me?"

Kevin and Jake looked at each other with fear in their eyes.

"Hell no! I'm not going in there. Are you guys crazy?" said Kevin.

"Fine, you stay here just in case someone comes. You let us know. We would let you know what we find. Jake, are you coming?"

"Okay, let's go."

Houdini went in first, making the ladder squeak with every step down. Jake followed after him.

Houdini was already down. He pointed the cell phone in every direction to see the place, but he really didn't have to see it to know what it looked like. The place was exactly as he had seen it or remembered it. The computers, the medical equipment, the operating table in the middle of the room, the room next door with the dividing glass window, the chair and monitor on the wall—everything was exactly as he remembered it. His hands were sweating. It felt like there was not enough oxygen in the room. He wasn't getting enough air in his lungs, and his heart was raising with fear.

"What is this place? How did you know?"

"It's a lab, an underground medical research lab." *A nightmare,* Houdini thought to himself. He felt like he was losing control again. He had to control it. He could not let the change take over now. *I'm in control, I'm in control,* he kept repeating in his mind. He took deep, slow breaths. He walked to the room next door. Jake followed behind him. On the other side of the wall, behind the glass window, was a file cabinet. They opened one of the drawers. It was full of papers—documents. He closed it and opened the one under it. He didn't know what he was looking for. But he was on a mission: to find anything that would explain who he was or where he had come from. He kept moving things around. There were medical equipment, syringes, papers. He was in the middle of opening the last bottom drawer when he heard Kevin scream.

"Hey, guys, hurry back up! I think I hear sirens. I think the police is on the way. Let's go!"

"Dude, let's go!" said Jake in a panic.

"Wait, we have time. It sounds far away." He opened the drawer and ran his fingers through the files. They seemed to be in alphabetical order. And right in front of his face, the first file read "Adam."

Houdini grabbed the file and put it under his shirt. "Let's go, quick! Move!"

They both ran as fast as they could out of the room. Papers and files were lining the floor around the file cabinet.

"Hurry, hurry!" they heard Kevin scream.

They reached the ladder and went up as fast as their legs could carry them. Once they got up, they ran toward the side door. The police sirens were louder and closer now. They left the building and ran into the woods. The side door to the building was still swinging when the police cars arrived.

But they did not bother looking back; they kept running through the back woods in the direction of the skating rink, the cold air hitting their faces, their hearts beating fast. But Houdini felt like he was in control this time. When they thought they were far enough from the warehouse, they made a turn from the back woods toward the sidewalk and kept running the rest of the way, looking back to make sure they were no being followed. They were exhausted by the time they reached the skating rink. And they got inside, sweating and panting.

"We didn't close the door to the lab," said Jake. "The police is going to find it."

"We had no choice. We had to get out of there before we were found out."

"But I think I got what I was looking for. We'll see."

A car horn interrupted the conversation. They looked out to see Mrs. Wellington's car waiting for them outside.

They got in the car and sat down. They were all quiet.

"Did you guys have a good time?"

"We did," Houdini replied, touching the file under his shirt, making sure it was not noticeable.

"Mom, do you think Jake can stay over tonight?"

"I don't see why not. It is up to his dad though."

They stayed up until late that night looking through the file and trying to decode the information in it. It was too complicated for them to understand it. They were mostly equations and medical terms. They would have to wait and research it a little more to find out what it meant.

"Hey, we should go back to the warehouse tomorrow in the daytime to see what else we find."

"Yeah, I guess we can do that. Let's just go to bed. I'm dead tired."

Chapter 15

The next morning, they woke up early and tried to leave the house before everyone else woke up. They went out back looking for the ATVs. There were only two ATVs and three of them, so Kevin and Jake would have to share the biggest of the two ATVs. The plan was to get to the warehouse through the back woods. Houdini knew the way well. Kevin and he had spent plenty of time riding through these woods.

"Guys, stop goofing around and let's go. We want to get there before daylight. We don't want to be seen," said Houdini.

It was a cold snowy morning. With the time change, even though it was around six in the morning, it was still black outside. The falling snow made it hard to see very far ahead, and the moist from their breath was clouding the glass in their helmet visor.

They had to ride slow because the snow was icy and got slippery at times. As they were approaching the back of the warehouse, they decided to leave the ATVs hidden in the woods and continue the rest of the way on foot. The noise of the ATVs got louder as they got closer to town. And the ATVs' trails kept getting narrower. Not too many people rode ATVs so close to town.

They kept walking through the snow the rest of the way. Walking was difficult. Their boots kept sinking in the snow, and they seemed to be getting heavier with every step.

"Great morning we picked to do this, bro," Kevin complained.

"I didn't know it would be snowing, and besides, it's not like we have a choice. We have to get to the documents before someone else does."

Even though the temperature was really low, they were sweating under their jackets.

When they got close enough to the building, they hid behind the bushes in the back of the warehouse until they were sure that there was no one around before they ventured into the building again.

Since it was still dark, it was hard to see from far away, so they started to walk slowly and cautiously toward the abandoned warehouse.

"Dude, there is police tape around the warehouse," said Jake, pointing in the direction of the building. "And look, the bathroom window has been boarded up."

"Shhhh! Lower your voice," whispered Houdini, pushing them both back into the bushes. "Look, there are lights inside the warehouse. It looks like flashlights. I think there are people inside."

They were trying to make sense of what was happening when they heard a loud voice coming from the warehouse.

"Who's there?"

Jake jumped back startled and stepped on a branch that broke beneath his snow boots, making a loud noise in the quiet of the early morning.

Before they knew what was happening, they saw two black shapes with flashlights running toward them.

The three of them took off running as fast as they could with the man following close behind them.

"Get them! Get them! Don't let them escape," they heard the man scream.

They were running fast toward the hidden ATV. If they could get to them in time, they would be home free. Running through the snow was very difficult. But they were younger and faster. They were almost to the ATVs when Houdini's boot got caught under a root or a branch, making him fall to the ground. Jake and Kevin noticed and tried to come back to help him get loose. But Houdini screamed to them to keep running.

"Go, go! I'm fine. I'll be fine. Get out of here! I'll catch up," said Houdini, trying to break free from whatever was holding him.

Jake and Kevin hesitated; they were not going to leave Houdini behind.

"Go, go, for real, dude! Go, get out of here."

Jake and Kevin made it to the ATVs and turned them on, the engines sounding real loud.

Houdini was still trying to get loose. He heard the whooshing of the man's boot in the snow. They were getting close, real close. His forehead was wet with perspiration, his heartbeat so loud he could feel it in his eardrums. His imagination was getting the best of him. He could see it now—being captured, taken to a lab again, being studied, probed with tools and injections, being locked in a cage in some strange lab, not being able to escape while they decided what to do with him. Terror got a hold of him. He was frozen with fear. He could hear the men breathing heavily. They were so close now. They would be next to him any minute.

In a last effort to free himself from whatever was holding him, he pulled his leg out of the snow boot and took off running with the two men following right behind. The snow felt really cold beneath his bare foot, but as bad as that was, the other boot was making it really difficult to run. The men were gaining distance; he could hear the engine of the ATVs ahead. They were waiting for him, he thought. Adrenaline was rushing through his body. *I have to stay in control, he thought to himself. I have to stay in control breath. Houdini, breathe.* He looked back to see the two men almost on him. He bent down, took off his other boot, and threw it on their direction, hitting one of them on the head and making him fall. The other one kept running after him. He heard Jake and Kevin scream in unison "Run, run, you can do it, run!"

The snow was very cold beneath his feet. And his feet kept sinking in the snow, making it very hard for him to advance, but fear kept him going as fast as he could. He kept slipping and falling in the parts where the snow had become icy. The guy that was left was gaining distance on him. He was reaching, trying to grab him. When finally he reached the clearing, Houdini mustered the last of his energy and sprinted toward the running ATVs.

"Give me your hand, give me your hand!" screamed Jake, reaching his hand out to him from the running ATV. With the man on his heels, Houdini grabbed Jake's hand and jumped on the back of the ATV, as Jake pressed on the gas, taking off so fast that it made the ATV jump.

Houdini looked back to see the last of the two men getting smaller in the distance.

*****

The man got back to the warehouse empty-handed and tired. They were met by two other men.

"They got away again," announced John.

"Do you think?" the older man asked sarcastically. He was also dressed in black and holding a flashlight. "We better get out of here before we are found out."

"Any news?"

"No, it seems that the police got here before we did. The door to the secret lab was open, and papers were scattered everywhere. It seems that the police or someone got hold of the files."

"Let's hope it's someone and not the police, or they would be knocking on our door soon."

"So what's the next move?" asked John as they were walking toward their car that was parked across the street from the warehouse, away from prying eyes.

"Well, we keep an eye on our boy/cat and wait for the right moment to capture him. We know where he leaves and the school he attends. I say we lie low until the heat dies out. But keep a very close eye on our boy and his friends."

"Will do, boss, will do."

Chapter 16

Well, Thanksgiving break was over. It was only a week, but it seemed as if a very long time had passed. So many things had happened that week, and now it was back to school as usual. He was going to have a very hard time focusing on school, he thought. It all seemed so trivial compared to all the other things that were happening in his life right now. But he welcomed the distraction. It would be good to be Houdini Wellington, a regular student at Jackson High, instead of the cat/boy, the baby boy embryo or Adam, like it said he was in the file he had found at the lab. It was all too complicated. He wanted to be like everyone else, to be just Houdini, and have a normal life like everyone else in school, without worrying about being followed or finding out who he was or where he came from.

He was looking forward to seeing Krissy again. That thought made him smile. He was daydreaming about her sweet face, not really looking where he was going, sort of like on autopilot, when he felt someone pushing him out of the way.

"Hey, freak, watch where you going."

When he looked up, his eyes met Keith's. "What is your problem?" he yelled back.

"You almost ran into me, you freak. That's the problem."

"Listen, I don't know what I ever did to you, but this has got to stop."

"Just don't like freaks, that's all," Keith said, walking in a menacing way toward Houdini. "I don't know what you're up to yet, but I'm going to find out. You don't fool me. I saw you and your nerd friends over at the warehouse district the other night. It makes me wonder what you guys were doing there. Usually people don't go there on weekends. I don't know what you losers are up to, but there's been some people asking questions around school this morning. I'm going to make it my job to make sure they find what they are looking for."

"Whatever," said Houdini, walking away without taking his eyes off Keith until Keith walked away. One thing he knew, he wasn't going to be intimidated. He knew how bullies were. They attack if they smell fear. He wasn't going to let Keith bully him. That's for sure.

But in home period, he couldn't stop thinking about what Keith had said. Was Keith following them? How did he know his whereabouts? And what Keith had said about people coming around inquiring about him worried him too. It got to be the same people that broke into the house. He thought, *But how did they know who I am, even down to my name?*

Who are these people, and what would they do to me once they got their hands on me?

That night he went to bed late. It had been a long day. He couldn't help but feel paranoid. After the altercation with Keith that day in school, he could not shake the feeling of being watched, of being followed. All day in school he kept getting up off his seat to look out the window for signs of people waiting outside of the school, or a strange car parked on the side of the road, waiting and watching. But fortunately, everything seemed to be normal.

On the way home from the bus stop, he kept watching over his shoulder while conversing with Kevin and trying to act nonchalant.

"Hey, are you okay?" asked Kevin. "You keep acting as if you're expecting something to happen. Is there something you are not telling me?"

He paused for a moment, deliberating whether to tell Kevin about what he heard from Keith. He didn't want to worry Kevin. But he needed to get it out of his chest, as if by sharing the fear, it will be easier to manage it.

Kevin listened quietly as Houdini told the story.

"Why do you think Keith is following us? What is it to him what we do? Or where we go?"

"I don't know. That's what I can't figure out, but what he said about people asking questions rang true to me. Those men at the warehouse were looking for something too. And I have the feeling I am it."

"Well, we have to be one step ahead of them always. We have to go back to the library, take all the document we have, and do some research. We have to get to the bottom of this. Whatever this is."

"Yep, you're right. Please don't tell Mom. I don't want to worry her more," said Houdini as they both walked quietly the rest of the way, both lost in thoughts.

Now it was past midnight, and Houdini could not fall as sleep. He kept turning the television on and off, staring at the ceiling, counting sheep. But nothing helped. He kept going over the events of the last days, reliving it in his mind's eyes, going over every conversation, trying to make sense of it all. It was past two when he finally fell asleep.

In this nightmare, he was in a dark room, in a cage. He was afraid. Through the cage door he saw a metal table. The moonlight coming through a window high up on the wall reflected on the table, making it shine. It was stainless steel, it seemed. On the table was a tray of medical equipment—syringe, scalpel, stethoscope, vials of medicine, etc. He was afraid. He was shaking; he had a terrible feeling that something was about to happen. He could smell it in the air. Suddenly the light turned on. He heard voices, steps approaching. He stepped back to the back of the cage. He felt the cool metal against his back. He was trembling. He could feel his heartbeat throbbing in his ears His eyes were trying to adjust to the light. His heart was beating hard. He let out a sound as he saw the white lab coat approaching the cage. But it was not a scream that came out of his mouth; it was a hiss. He was a cat. He was trying to process the thought when the door to the cage opened and a hand reached for him. He was trying to avoid it but couldn't. The hand grabbed him hard. He swirled and arched, trying to get loose. He clawed at the hand, but the hand was wrapped around him, holding him tight, too tight. He saw a face coming into view. He was struck with fear. He has seen that face before; he knew that face, but where? Where?

He woke up, heart pounding out of his chest and wet with perspiration. He was in his room. He was safe. He looked around, making sure. Yes, he was safe… for now, he thought.

Chapter 17

It was a gloomy and snowy winter morning. They had too many mornings like this this winter, too many to count. *This winter is looking to be a harsh, long winter*, Mrs. Wellington thought as she looked through the window of the diner to the snow-covered streets. The white snow was glistening in the moonlight. It was beautiful and peaceful at this time. There weren't many car track marks on the road yet, since it was so early in the morning and people were not up yet. Soon the snowplow would go through, making way for cars to go by. It had snowed so much this winter that the snow accumulated on the side of the road in high piles. There had not been enough sunny days to melt the snow before the next snowfall, and the salt was running low. The snow made the streets almost look like a tunnel. In the news, meteorologists were predicting lots of flooding for the next spring when the snow began to melt. One more thing to worry about, she thought. It was her turn to open the diner and get it ready for the breakfast rush, even though she doubted that a lot of people would show up for breakfast with the current weather condition. Even the schools were closed today.

Nonetheless she started a pot of coffee and began to put the clean tablecloths back on the tables. Better to be ready, she thought, unlocking the front door. After pouring a cup of coffee for herself, she sat on a table close to the window, newspaper in hand, ready to catch up with the news. When she opened the paper, the headlines caught her attention right away. There, in first page the headlights, read, "Local Warehouse Raid," and it showed a picture of a warehouse in town surrounded by yellow police crime tape. Her pulse accelerated. She had a feeling that somehow this had something to do with Houdini. Call it mother's intuition, she thought.

She continued reading. Apparently, the police had followed a tip to discover an abandoned science laboratory near the warehouse district. The place has been used, by the looks of it, as an illegal underground experimental lab. It was suspected to be connected to animal abuse. More investigation was needed. It read, "But the case had been turned to the FBI. So far they have no suspects." She stopped reading. She didn't need to know the rest of it. It was all becoming real clear to her. The lab, the animal experiments, the cat showing up at the Humane Society out of nowhere, the sign on the cat's collar, the break-in at the house next door, the cat turning human—it all made sense to her now. These scientists, whoever they were, at that lab had somehow created Houdini. And now they were trying to get rid of the evidence, which meant Houdini himself. He was the only telltale of their illegal activities, and they were trying to destroy it to cover their tracks.

Blood was rushing to her head, and she felt dizzy. She had to hold onto a chair nearby to keep herself from collapsing on the floor. Houdini was in danger, she realized, and she needed to protect him. She felt a pain in her chest. She knew at that moment that she would protect him with her own life if necessary. They would have to walk over her dead body to get to him.

*****

Kevin's cell phone rang. He woke up with the vibration on the nightstand. He was half asleep and disoriented. He almost dropped the phone as he tried to grab it.

"Hello?" he answered, sounding sleepy.

"Kev, it's Mom. Are you guys okay?"

Kevin looked at the alarm clock sitting on the nightstand next to his bed. The small numbers on the radio alarm clock shone too bright, bothering his sleepy eyes. He had to squint to see it. It showed the time to be 5:30 a.m.

"What? Mom? What are you doing calling so early? There is not even school today."

"Is Houdini okay?"

"Yes, Mom, why wouldn't he be? What?"

"Do me a favor, Kev. Go over to his room and wake him up. Tell him to watch the six o'clock news on TV. Both of you watch it. We will talk later, and make sure all the doors are locked."

"Mom, what's wrong?"

"Just do it! I'll be home later. We will talk."

Kevin and Houdini went down to the family room, turned on the television, and sat on the sofa not knowing what to expect. The news anchor, a middle-aged woman with too much makeup on, talk about the traffic on Highway 75 and what to expect if you were traveling to work. Apparently, the snow and black ice were causing delays. They moved on to schools being closed due to the snow, then the national unemployment rate, etc. They were about to go back to bed when the anchor said, "And moving on to local news…" and then they saw it. A picture of the warehouse was shown on the TV screen. They recognized it right away. And then the story followed: "The case had been turned to the FBI for investigation, and now PETA [People for the Ethical Treatment of Animals] is putting pressure on the police to solve the case."

Houdini finished watching the rest of the news in disbelief.

The cat was out of the bag! He laughed at the irony. It was just a matter of time now before everything would be brought to the light, but what was that exactly? He didn't even know himself. People were after him, he knew that, but why?

He ran to his room and took the files he had gotten from the warehouse out of the drawer where he had hidden them. Time was running out. He need it to know what he was against so he could defend himself if needed. He grabbed his cell phone and dialed Jake's number. Jake's sleepy voice answered on the other end.

"Huh?"

"Jake, I need you to come over as soon as possible. Is your dad home?"

"What? What happened?"

"It's a long story. I will fill you in when you get here. Can you come?"

"Sure…"

Chapter 18

All three of them were sitting on the floor of Houdini's room, papers spread all around them. They had been sitting there for at least two to three hours, and they still hadn't figured out one thing. The papers were written in medical terminology that was too intricate for the common person to understand. There were lots of symbols and mathematical equation. Houdini's stomach was growling. They hadn't had any breakfast yet. They decided to take a break from the file and all the papers. Maybe they would see things in a different light once they stepped away from it for a while.

Anna was in the kitchen when they got there. She was making waffles. Breakfast was usually big on Saturday morning. Mrs. Wellington made sure of it. Breakfast was family time. She didn't get to spend a lot of time with the kids with the crazy schedule she had at the diner. So she made sure the kids would wake up to the smell of bacon and pancakes on Saturday morning, a welcome break from the usual bowl of cereal they had during the weekdays. Even though it wasn't Saturday, Anna had taken upon herself to make breakfast this morning since Mrs. Wellington wasn't there, and there was no school that day.

"What were you guys doing upstairs for so long?"

"Nothing, guys stuff. You wouldn't understand," said Houdini absentmindedly.

"Wow! Really? I think I liked you better when you were a cat." Anna waited for a reply but got nothing. She shook her head in disbelief, turned around, and tended to the waffle maker that was beeping, letting her know it was time to flip it over.

They were all in their own thoughts, trying to figure out Houdini's origin and the mystery that surrounded it. Figuring things out had proven to be more difficult than they ever anticipated. There had to be some information out there about it. Someone had to know something.

He would skip lunch on Monday at school and take all the papers they had to the school library, he thought. He had two days until then. He would lie low, stay out of sight, and hope that no one would come around trying to find him. Now there was something else he needed to do. He needed to figure out how to control his emotions. He needed to be in charge of when and where he would change into a cat. So far he had been able to stop it from happening. He was happy about that. But he needed to know how to make it happen at will. That was the only way he was going to be in control.

They were out by the woods behind the house. They had taken out the ATVs. Kevin and Jake rode the ATVs while Houdini ran next to it, trying to keep up.

"Dude, stop! Stop!" yelled Houdini, bending over, trying to catch his breath. He was wearing jean joggers without a shirt, and drops of sweat dripped from his forehead into his eyes, making them sting. His muscular back was also glistening with sweat.

"We have been doing this awhile, and nothing is happening," said Houdini, sitting and resting his back against a big oak tree. He exhaled. "I don't think this is going to work."

"What do you mean?" said Kevin. "This is the way it happened before. Remember when the dog chased you that day when we were coming home from school? You were running then."

"And the time we were being chased by the men close to the lake, you were running then too," Jake joined in.

"It's not working." Houdini closed his eyes and rested his head against the tree. He was exhausted.

"What then? Think, what other time did it happen?"

He was going back in his thoughts, trying to remember. The first time it happened he had not been aware of it. He woke up remembering nothing in that abandoned house. It had taken days for him to remember who he was. That was not going to help. The other time had been at the movie theater when he confronted Keith. But that time it had only been the eyes that changed.

"Dude, I got it! It has to be fear. Think about it. You were afraid of the dog chasing you. Who wouldn't be? That dog was vicious."

"And you were afraid of being caught by those men at the lake. Who's to know what they would've done to you if they caught you," said Jake.

"I was not afraid."

"Yes, you were! We were all afraid."

The more they talked about it, the more sense it made.

Fear, Houdini thought to himself. If that was the case, controlling it was going to be more difficult than he expected. How does one control fear? Fear is circumstantial, and who can control what will happen? He felt defeated.

In bed that night, he was restless. It's funny how things that happen during the day become ten times bigger when everyone is asleep and you are alone on your bed. Things that seem manageable during the day somehow seem nearly impossible to solve when you are left all alone with your thoughts. He had plenty of experience with sleepless nights, trying to remember his past or waking up from a bad nightmare. There were times when he couldn't figure out if they were actual nightmares or his past trying to resurface, his brain remembering things he could not.

He lay in bed, eyes fixed on the ceiling, aware of every little noise the house made. He tried to recall everything he ever heard about fear: There is nothing to fear but fear itself. Being brave is not the absent of fear, but doing what's right in spite of the fear.

"Fear not for I am with you," he read once in the Bible, nothing that will help him, he thought. He didn't need to control fear—he needed to make fear happen.

As he drifted asleep, he saw himself in the same cage he had been before. He saw the hand reaching for him, grabbing him. He fought with all his strength, twisting and scratching, trying to get loose. He had been pinned to the metal table. Two people in white lab coats were holding him as he struggled and lashed out under their hands. He hissed and meowed; he felt helpless. One of the men reached for a medicine tube sitting at the tray next to him. Houdini's heart was racing uncontrollably. The other man held Houdini's head up, his hands clutching the cat's mouth. Houdini was not able to hiss or make any kind of noise; he was looking straight at the man now. The man's face was concealed by the surgical mask he wore.

The second person opened the tube's cap and squeezed something on his finger. He saw the hand go straight to his face. *Oh no!* he thought. His body hairs were standing up, and his ears were back so low he could feel them against the back of his head. He tried to break free, but the hands were holding him tight. He saw the finger come to his eyes; he felt something gooey going in them. His eyes were stinging badly, and his heart was pounding out of his chest. He tried to see.

Everything was blurry. But he felt he was moving. They were moving him. He was horrified. He was being lowered down. He didn't know to where, but his stomach had butterflies in it, like the one you get in an elevator going down, or better yet, a roller coaster. He tried to fight to break free from the hands that were holding him. He fought with all his strength, but they were gripping him too hard. His paws touched something cold, wet... his brain was trying to register what it was. He could not see.

It was water or some kind of liquid, he thought in horror, right before he was submerged in it. It was freezing cold. His body tried to take a breath in, from the shock of the freezing water, but his brain knew he couldn't breathe. He held his breath. His body felt cold, freezing cold. It was dark. He tried frantically to break loose, but he was held tightly underwater. He needed air in his lungs. His lungs were burning, hurting. He was terrified. He thought he would pass out. And then he woke up, his back against the headboard of his bed, bedsheets in a bundle by his feet, near the foot of the bed. He looked around, breathing heavily, still scared, and then he cried. He could not control his sobs, his heart still raising out of control. He kept crying hard. This was no dream; this was a memory. He was sure of it.

The next morning he was up before everyone in the house. The memories of the dream were fresh in his mind. He had made a decision. He was going to use the fear he had felt the night before to take control of his metamorphosis. He sneaked out of the house, being careful not to make loud noises. He didn't want anyone to see him leave or follow him.

He needed to do this alone. This was something he needed to do on his own. Anyone else would be a distraction. He went past the house and into the woods; it was about six in the morning. The sun wasn't out yet. It had been a moonless night. But visibility wasn't a problem for Houdini. He could see at night as good as day. He kept walking through the trees until he reached a clearing. He felt exposed then, vulnerable. A thought crossed his mind that made him second-guess if his decision to leave the house without telling anyone had been a good one.

What if the people that were after him had been watching the house? What if they knew that he was alone out there? He would be an easy prey. *I'll take my chances,* he thought to himself.

Fear was creeping up on him. He felt his blood turning cold. He would use this to his advantage. Fear is what he needed right now. He closed his eyes and tried hard to concentrate on the memories from last night's dream. He tried to relive every moment of it. The nightmare was still very vivid in his mind. The pain in his eyes, not being able to breathe, his heart started to race. His body was trembling, and then something else kicked in, feelings he didn't even know he had. A flood of emotions washed over him like a tsunami. Anger. He was *mad*. Mad at the people that had done this to him, at the injustice of it all. He hadn't asked for any of this. He was robbed from all the memories of his past. Even though now that he was remembering, he was not sure he wanted them. Was he always a cat? Or was he human? And if he was human, then he was robbed of his childhood, of his rights, of having a biological family, of the opportunity of having a normal life. They had made him into a freak. He had been abused and hurt, and why? Why him? He didn't deserve any of it.

All the rage he felt at the moment exploded in his insides. He felt blood rushing to his head. Rage was washing over him like an ocean wave. Even though it was winter, he felt heat all over his body, and then it happened. He opened his eyes and looked down at his feet; they were now two back hairy paws. He looked both ways to make sure no one was around. And then he ran. He felt very light and agile. The snow somehow didn't feel cold against his paws. All his senses were magnified. He could see clearer than ever; he could smell things he had never smelled before, scents that were coming from far away carried by the wind. He could hear the smallest of noise, the leaves rustling in the trees, a beetle walking across the ground. It was intoxicating. And even though he was just a cat, he felt strong and powerful and free.

He ran for a while, feeling the wind rush through his fur. He climbed trees, mesmerized at how effortless it felt. He could jump from high up on the trees and fall back on his paws again and again. He tried hunting small mammals just to see how fast he was. Of course he didn't kill them. It was just for practice.

He spent most of the day changing forms, from human to cat and back to human again. He channeled all the fear and the rage that he felt inside to make it happen. After changing back and forward time and time again, he felt accomplished. He had mastered it. Now he could use it at will.

He looked up at the sky. It was a clear day. There wasn't a cloud in the blue/gray winter sky. He could not wait for summer. The sun was shining high up in the middle of the sky. He knew it would be around 12:30 or 1:00; he had to get back home. His family must be worried by now. He didn't want to cause them more stress.

He jumped, grabbed a tree branch, snapped it from the pine tree, bent down, and brushed it over the snow, erasing the pawprints just in case, he thought to himself.

Monday morning was finally here. Time to go back to school. He woke up earlier than usual and turned on the television. He was not sure if school would still be on or canceled due to the black ice that had collected on the roads the last couple of days. He was hoping today wouldn't be another snow day, or they could lose their winter break in February to make up for lost time.

Every day at school that week he looked over his shoulder, making sure he wasn't followed. He was also surprised not to see Keith anywhere in school. *He must be sick with the flu that's going around,* he thought, but he welcomed the opportunity of not having to deal with him. He spent time with Jake and Krissy every chance he had. They sat together at lunch and hung out. The thought of coming clean to Krissy was tugging at his heart. They had gotten very close. He felt they could talk about everything. And yet she didn't know the most important thing about him.

She didn't know who he was. Would she love him the same if she knew he was a freak? A cat-boy? He felt like a fraud. But he had to think about this real carefully before he told anyone else. His life was at risk. Besides, what if she rejected him? That would be more than he could take. He didn't want to even think about that. Every day after school he would go back in the woods and change into a cat. He had done it so many times that now it took no effort at all. It was second nature at this point. He ran free through the woods. He hunted small creatures—squirrels, chipmunks, birds, mouse, anything he could use for agility practice. He felt free and strong. He loved being out there in cat form, except for the encounters he sometimes had with neighborhood dogs, who furiously pursued him in an attempt to attack him. He would have to run up a tree and wait for them to lose interest and leave, before he was able to come down from the tree and go home. But even that, he used to test his abilities. It made him run faster, act quickly, think fast, and stay in control. He used all of it to become better, stronger.

In his human form, he noticed his body was changing also. He was becoming stronger, more muscular, more athletic. His reflexes were very acute now, and so was his night vision. One afternoon after school, while playing football with Jake and Kevin at the school yard, he was asked by the track-and-field coach to join his team after seeing him run. The coach seemed to be very impressed with his speed.

Nothing else had happened regarding the warehouse or the files. And nothing had been in the news lately about the investigation into the case. He was glad to be able to be a normal kid for once. But still, sometimes late at night in his room, he had a feeling that he was being watched. Sometimes the hairs on the back of his neck would stand up for no apparent reason. And he found himself checking all the windows and doors to make sure he was safe. His nightmares were still going strong.

One morning toward the middle of December, after a major snowstorm, they woke up to find fresh footprints around the back door and windows. And they knew right then and there that the nightmare wasn't over. They were still being watched. They were still trying to get to Houdini.

Sitting at the breakfast table, they disused what to do about it.

"I don't think we should call the police again. After all the publicity on the news, I don't want to give any reason for them to start asking questions. How are we going to explain Houdini's presence if they really dig into it?"

"Mom, how will they know anything about Houdini? You are being paranoid."

"I don't know, Kevin. They would ask question. Do we have any enemies? Do we know anyone who wants to hurt us? And what would I say? I think they are after my son because he is a cat? Do you hear how ridiculous that sounds?"

"Mom, it will be fine. Don't worry, I'll be safe. We just have to be prepared for anything, be alert, that's all. So far they haven't tried anything drastic."

"But what if they do, Houdini? What then? To whom do we go for help?"

"We have the shotgun that Kevin's dad gave him for his birthday. We can use it for protection if anyone breaks into the house."

"Mom, I'm afraid." Anna scooted closer to her mom, holding her hand.

"Don't be, sweetie. We will be fine. I'm calling alarm companies today. We'll get an alarm system for the house."

"But what if they take Houdini?"

"Don't worry about me, Anna. They won't get to me. I know they are coming. I know I'm being followed. I'm prepared. Besides, I'm really fast. I can change forms. They won't get me, I promise." The words brought him no comfort, but he hoped they might ease the worry he could hear in his sister's voice.

"Houdini, do you remember anything from your previous life at all?" At this, everyone's eyes were on Houdini.

"No, Anna, I don't remember much, and what I remember, I wish I could forget."

"Well, you have us now, and we love you."

"I know, honey. I know."

Chapter 19

His life hadn't been easy, Keith thought. He was born addicted to alcohol, thanks to his alcoholic mother, who didn't stop drinking regardless of being pregnant with him. She was actually inebriated as she had delivered him. He was born smaller than most babies, and his lungs were undeveloped. He spent a month in the hospital's neonatal unit, hooked up to machines. After, life hadn't been any better. He'd been in many homeless shelters through the years. Every time his mother wasn't able to pay the rent, they got evicted. He had seen plenty of abuse from his drunk mom and his mom's constant parade of boyfriends. He had been bullied all his life, and now it was he who was a bully to others. Putting other people down made him feel better somehow. He wanted to inflict on other some of the pain that was given to him. He knew deep inside that they didn't deserve it. But so what? Neither did he. And no one ever cared. Houdini was his new target. He didn't know why, but he had rubbed him the wrong way since the first time he saw him. He could see something special and different about Houdini, something he knew he didn't have, and that made him feel inferior. He hated that feeling. He had felt inferior all his life. He had always looked the wrong way or worn the wrong clothes or lived in the wrong side of the tracks. People had always looked down on him. He always felt belittled and worthless. And someone had to pay for that. Houdini was as good of a target as any. And now, thanks to those people, he had a chance to even out the score.

The two men had come around the school, asking questions about Houdini, and he had been more than happy to provide them with all the information he had on him. When was the first time he had seen him in school? Where he lived and how he had seen Houdini and his friends around the warehouse district that one night. They had offered to pay him for anything else he could find out about Houdini, which made the deal that much sweeter. He would've done it for free, Keith thought to himself and smiled.

Now he was on the case; he was going to become Houdini's shadow until he could find anything of substance to relay to his predators.

*****

Christmas season was approaching. Streets were decorated, stores were full, and Christmas music played constantly on the radio. Houdini had gotten a seasonal job at the mall as Santa's elf.

For now he had put his worries aside and was concentrating on his own teenage life. There would be plenty of time to investigate his origins. That part of his existence wasn't going to change. He and Krissy hadn't seen each other over two weeks now, and she was the only thing that occupied his mind. Thanks to Krissy's father, who had decided that Krissy was too young to be in such intense relationship. They hadn't been able to even talk on the phone. The two weeks of winter break had been tough. Her phone was taken away. Through Jake he let Krissy know to meet him at the mall. He was waiting for her at the food court. His heart leapt when he saw her walking toward him. He couldn't believe how he had gotten so lucky as to land a girl like her. Her big green eyes shone with joy when they finally hugged.

Chapter 20

Christmas Day was finally here. The house was fully decorated for the season. Mrs. Wellington took a lot of pride in her Christmas décor. It had taken her three days to get the house ready for Christmas, from the Christmas wreaths hanging in every room to the Department 56 snow village she displayed in the family room next to the tree. It had been a family tradition to set it up together every year. It was hard work and it took half the room, but once it was set, it was beautiful to watch, and it definitely set the tone for the celebration. The stockings were hung on the fireplace, and the Christmas tree they had gone to pick as a family a couple of weeks earlier gleamed in a corner of the family room. Handmade ornaments that Kevin and Anna had made throughout the years held a special place among the fancy store-bought ornaments. A reindeer head that Anna had made in kindergarten made out of construction foam with googly eyes was one of Mrs. Wellington's favorite, and a Thanksgiving turkey made out of pine cone that Kevin had made in the second grade also had a spotlight on the family Christmas tree.

Houdini's heart was filled with sadness. He thought about how different life would have been for him if he had been allowed to have a biological family, the family he had a right to belong and was stolen from him, a regular childhood like everyone else. Maybe in some house, in some family's Christmas tree his handmade ornaments would be proudly displayed too. It wasn't fair, he thought as his eyes filled up with tears. He took a deep breath, trying hard to control his emotions. The last thing he wanted was to turn into a cat right now as he wiped the tears from his eyes. Something on the Christmas tree caught his attention, and then he saw it. Hanging from one of the tree branches in a very visible spot was a cat's collar with the name Adam monogramed on it.

Anna, running down the stairs, startled him.

"Mom, wake up! It's Christmas morning. Kev, come see what we got."

Kevin came down the stairs, yawning and rubbing the sleep out of his eyes.

"I'm here, Anna," said Mrs. Wellington from the kitchen. "I got an early start on Christmas breakfast."

"Can we open the presents now, Mom, pleaseeee."

"Don't you want to eat first, honey?"

"No, Mom, please, I'm not that hungry. Just one, please."

Mrs. Wellington laughed. "Okay, sweetie, just one, but let me go over there so I can see your face when you open it." She walked over, drying her hands on her apron.

"How about this one, Anna?" said Houdini, pointing at a box under the tree, back against the wall. "I think it has your name on it."

"Yeah, that's a big one. Give me that one."

Houdini grabbed the box and carefully handed it over to Anna. They were all sitting around the Christmas tree now.

"Wait a minute, let's do this right," said Kevin, getting up to get his cell phone. "It's the first gift of Christmas. We have to document it and put it in social media."

"And we need music too, Christmas music, to make it official."

"And now drummer rolls…"

Anna looked down at the box. It read, "To Anna, from Santa, just kidding, Houdini."

Anna ripped the wrapping paper as fast as she could and opened the box. Her face full of excitement turned to surprise when she saw what was inside the box, or better yet, coming out of the box was a fluffy white kitten.

Anna's eyes filled up with tears. "What? This is awesome!" she screamed with excitement, trying to get the little kitten's claws off her shirt. The kitten was meowing and frantically trying to hold on.

"Thanks, Houdini," she said, hugging him so tight he could hardly breathe. "This is the best present ever!"

"Just make sure it's an actual cat this time," said Kevin. "This family is getting way too big."

"Hilarious, bro," replied Houdini, punching him on the shoulder. "Ha ha!"

For the New Year, Houdini invited Jake over to spend the night since his dad was out of town on business. They watched scary movies and ate popcorn, trying to stay awake until midnight in Kevin's room so they could toast to the New Year, with apple cider of course, while Mrs. Wellington and Anna watched on TV the celebration in Times Square, waiting for the ball to drop. But Houdini was more interested on the fireworks Kevin had been saving since Fourth of July than the beginning of the new year. Tonight, at 12:01, they were planning on sneaking into the woods where they had set up the fireworks. They had bottles lined up all over, holding the fireworks. They were trying to stay under his mother's radar for this. They knew where she stood on fireworks. Way too dangerous. One could lose a hand or an eye. They heard it many times before.

Once the new year started, there were going to be so many fireworks going on at the same time that she would not be able to tell where they were coming from or who was responsible for it. They waited about five minutes after twelve. After they exchanged hugs and kisses and toasted to the New Year, Mrs. Wellington went to bed, and out the back door went Jake, Kevin, and Houdini, being very careful of not being noticed. Once they passed the backyard, they ran the rest of the way into the woods to where they had hidden the fireworks. The night was one of the coldest night of this winter so far, and it was a moon-less night, but none of that bothered them. Better, they thought. It would make the fireworks look brighter. Once they got to the clearing, they got busy setting up the firework.

Other fireworks were going up in the sky from different directions. The loud noise was beginning to bother Houdini's sensitive hearing. It was too much noise, too intense, too loud for his feline ears. He started to get an uneasy feeling he could not shake. The little hair on the back of his neck started to prick up. A chill went up and down his back. He sensed danger. He motioned to the other two to be quiet. They stood still for a minute, and then he heard it. Even over the loud noise of the fireworks, he could hear steps approaching in different directions. He could hear the rustle of pants rubbing between the legs of people walking. He heard the crashing noise of the ice under boots, and his heart sank to his stomach. He turned around slowly to see three men dressed in black, with black mask covering their faces, approaching them in the dark. Houdini could see per-fectly well that they were holding a gun. Perspiration began to form on his forehead and upper lip. He made a signal to the others. They looked straight at each other's eyes and didn't feel a need to talk. The men were closing in slowly, trying not to be seen or heard. Houdini's heart was beating hard and fast. His blood was cold; his legs were shaking. The men were almost there, so close he could smell them. He made the sign again—one finger, then two, then three.

And the three of them all took off running in different directions, trying to confuse the men. It worked. The men froze in place for a minute, not knowing what to do. Then they took off running after them.

"Get the cat!" one of them screamed. "Forget the others, just get the cat."

Houdini was running as fast as his legs could carry him, zigzagging between the trees, trying to avoid the bullets from the men firing guns. They meant business this time. They didn't care about the gunshot sounds on a night like this. No one would notice it. The gunshots would be confused with the noise from the fireworks. No one would be the wiser. All kinds of thoughts were going through Houdini's mind. Was Kevin okay? Was Jake? He had no problem seeing where he was going in the dark, but it was so dark for the other two. *What if they had been captured?* He had to keep running away from the guns. Adrenaline was pumping through his body, his brain thinking about a mile a minute. He had to lure these men away from the house, away from his sleeping, defenseless mom and from Anna. He could go up a tree, that would be easy for him to do, but somehow he knew that that was exactly what his persecutor were expecting him to do, to follow his cat instincts and climb a tree. He would be a sitting duck then. All the men would have to do would be just to sit and wait for him to climb down. That is, if they wanted to capture him alive. He wasn't so sure anymore.

They were following close; he could hear their voices. One of the bullets flew real close to his ear, making a hissing sound. He had to act fast. He made a fast turn away from the house toward the street. People were out tonight, driving home from parties and get-togethers. Someone was bound to see him running, to see him being followed, being shot at. The busy street was his only chance. He tried to run faster. From afar he could see a car parked by the curb. The light of the car flashed on as he was approaching the street, and the engine started. *Good,* he was thinking. *It saw me.* His leg muscles were about to give out. As he got on the street to flag the car down, his leg muscle twitching from running and trying to catch his breath, the headlights from the car blinded him. He froze, not knowing what to do. The car was accelerating; it was charging toward him. *No,* he thought, paralyzed with fear. He raised his hands in front of his face for shelter, preparing for impact, when he felt someone pushing him out of the car's way. It all went down too fast for his brain to realize what was happening. His knees hit the pavement, and then his forehead right after. He was facedown on the asphalt. Then he heard screeching noises, the car tires rubbing on the asphalt.

He looked up to see the car swerving to the left to avoid hitting whoever was standing between him and the car, and then driving fast down the street and into the night. He was disoriented for a minute. His eyes were beginning to adjust to the dark again and then…

"Are you okay? Are you hurt?" came a voice he recognized instantly.

"Jake, are you crazy? What you do, bro? You could've been killed." He looked at him in disbelief. "Did you just jump in front of a moving car to save my life?… Are you okay?"

He got up, dusting the gravel from his knee. Extending his arm, he pulled Jake to his feet. They stood there in the middle of the street, both of them too shaken to even talk. Sweat droplets were running from Houdini's back. His shirt soaked to his back's skin.

Kevin came running out of the bushes into the street. "Are you guys okay? What happened? Are they gone?" They looked both ways down the street. No sign of car coming or going. It didn't seem like anyone was following them anymore. They looked up to see the fireworks still illuminating the dark winter sky. A cloud of smoke seemed to be covering everything now, and the smell of explosives was very strong. They let the night air fill their lungs, feeling happy to be alive. Then carefully they started to walk back home, too tired to even talk, the unused fireworks long forgotten in the woods.

Chapter 21

The new year began with a bang. Houdini woke up to Mrs. Wellington glued to the TV set. She had woken up early as usual to go to the diner and turned on the news. She always liked to see about the first baby born on New Year. And to her surprise, she saw way more than she was prepared for. It seemed like the pressure from PETA about getting to the bottom of the investigation into the supposed animal abuse in the local warehouse had finally paid off, and the policed investigation had yield some interesting facts. According to public records,

With the cloning of a sheep known as Dolly in 1996 by somatic cell nuclear transfer (SCNT), the idea of human cloning became a hot debate topic. Many nations outlawed it, while a few scientists promised to make a clone within the next few years. The first hybrid human clone was created in November 1998, by Advanced Cell Technology.

162

> It was created using SCNT—a nucleus was taken from a man's leg cell and inserted into a cow's egg from which the nucleus had been removed, and the hybrid cell was cultured, and developed into an embryo. The embryo was destroyed after 12 days.

That's what the article read, but according to the police investigation, the so-called embryo was not one but two. And according to undisclosed police records of the time, one of the embryos was stolen from the lab. At the time, the police investigated the case to the fullest. They investigated everyone involved in the experiment—from the scientists to the lab workers to the ambulance drivers and nurses. They followed every lead they had on the case but were not able to prove any wrongdoing or make any arrest. The investigation into the disappearance of the embryo was not made known to the public for fear of the bad publicity and the repercussions this would bring, since the topic was taboo. They figured that even if the embryo was stolen, there wasn't much anyone could do with it, so they dropped the case.

Now, with the discovery of the undercover lab and the rumors of animal abuse and experimentation with animals, the police had opened a new investigation on the case just in case the two of them were related somehow.

After they all watched that part of the news report that Mrs. Wellington had recorded, they all sat down in silence. The heaviness of the situation was beginning to sink in. None of them wanted to admit it, but they all knew deep inside what this meant, especially Houdini, who was as white as paper and staring straight at the television set like in a trance. They all knew what the police didn't even know yet. Houdini was the missing embryo that was stolen from the lab so many years back, an embryo that was genetically altered and apparently mixed with cat DNA.

Everything was clear now—how the cat had mysteriously appeared at the Humane Society in the middle of the night, the cat collar that the cat had been wearing when found, the name on the cat's collar, Adam. The first human being was named Adam, according to the Bible. It only made sense that the first cloned embryo would be named Adam as well. All the documents they had gotten from the warehouse and were unable to decode were about that too. The DNA strand with the letter b in the center, the B stands for "boy" or "boy embryo."

All these thoughts were running through Houdini's mind. It was too much to take in all at once. He felt dizzy. No one dared to talk.

*****

It took Houdini a while to come to terms with the reality of the situation. He spent the next few days locked in his room, not willing to talk to anyone, refusing the food that Mrs. Wellington left in front of his room's door, and even refusing to go to school, which had resumed on January 2, right after the Christmas break or winter break like some people like to call it these days. In his mind he always knew he had a sketchy beginning to his life. But now it was all too real and weird. If what they knew or suspected to be the truth turned out to be actually true, he was the embryo stolen from the lab. He was the only one of his kind on the whole planet. There was no one else alive that shared his DNA. He was an experiment gone wrong, a mistake that others were trying to correct or eliminate. That's why he had people after him trying to end his life in an effort to clear their tracks, their involvement in something that never should have happened in the first place. His very existence was illegal and unethical, the result of humans playing God.

And what about the many other questions that would never be answered? Like how long will he live? Would he age like regular people? Does he have nine lives? The thought of that one made him smile for a brief second, thinking of the irony of it all. But back to reality... Would he be able to have a family one day? Like regular people do? Would he end up turning into a cat, or would he remain mostly human? His brain went on and on all day and kept him up most of the nights.

All these questions would never be answered, he came to realize. Even if the scientists who stole the embryo and created him would be apprehended by the police and made to pay for what they had done, it would not change a thing about his life. He was sure of it. Even the people that created him wouldn't have an answer to any of his questions. He was a freak of nature, an enigma.

And what would happen if people outside of his circle found out about him? What then? The press would surely be all over the story. The medical community would probably like to experiment on him. Scientists from all over the world would be fighting for a chance to study the cat-boy, the human cat. God knows what he would be put through in the name of science or for the benefit of the human race.

He will never be allowed to lead a "normal" life. He scoffed at the thought. There was nothing normal about his life. He might as well be an alien, a mermaid, a unicorn—it didn't matter.

Emotions overwhelmed him, and he threw himself back on the bed, crying in desperation.

Chapter 22

Keith always knew he wasn't the sharpest tool in the box. People always made a point of letting him know that. But he recognized a good opportunity when he saw one, and this was it. He had spent some time following Houdini now. As told by the strangers that had shown up at school asking questions about Houdini, he knew all of Houdini's whereabouts. He even had gotten paid for letting those people know about Houdini's location on New Year's Eve. He didn't know exactly what interest they had on a loser like Houdini, but he didn't care much about Houdini, and he was getting paid for it, so whatever. He didn't ask too many questions. In situations like this, the least you know the better. Too much information can get you killed. Now, however, after seeing the news coverage on the local warehouse raid case, he was beginning to understand what was going on. He always thought that there was something wrong about Houdini, but he was never able to put his finger on it. He had been thinking back, going over everything he knew about Houdini—him being so jumpy, so skittish, so agile, so ADD-ish (if that was even a word), always distracted. He was always going around with his other loser friend, snooping around the school library, looking at weird books and searching on the computer for God knows what. It was all too weird.

He remembered their encounter at the movie theater that one time when he could swear he saw Houdini's eyes turn into some kind of animal's eyes. He didn't know what any of it meant. But obviously, there had to be a reason why important looking people were willing to pay for information on the loser. And information was valuable these days if people were willing to pay for it. He was sure others would pay more for the same information. Maybe he should skip the whole dealing with this people and go straight to the news with what he knew. Hey, he might even become a local celebrity for it. But what did he know exactly?

*****

After a week of seclusion and self-pity, Houdini woke up and jumped out of bed, ready to face reality. He realized that there was nothing he could do to change the facts, and wallowing in self-pity wasn't going to solve anything. He watched his own reflection in the bathroom mirror. He looked different, he thought to himself. Yes, he looked tired, and there were dark circles under his eyes for lack of sleep. But that wasn't what made him look different. It was something in his eyes, a maturity that wasn't there before. He looked older, wiser somehow, like he had been forced to grow up in one week. He stared at his own reflection in the mirror. He was muscular and pale. Human. Definitely no one would be able to tell any different by looking at him. His big green almond-shaped eyes were his face's most prominent feature, and his jet-black hair of course. He added some hair gel to it to make it spike. He took one more look in the mirror, threw his infamous black sweatshirt on, grabbed his book bag from a chair next to the window, and headed out the door.

Whatever the day was going to bring, he was ready for it. Not used in hiding either. He just had to be extra careful, be wiser, stay one step ahead of things. The main goal was not to be found out, not to be captured. He knew what would happen if he did. His very own life depended on it.

When he arrived at school, Krissy was waiting for him in their usual hung-out place. The minute she saw him, she ran toward him and threw her arms around him. "Oh my god, where have you been? Why didn't you answer your phone? I must've called at least a hundred times. You okay? Jake said you weren't answering his text either. Are you okay?"

He felt like answering, "No, I'm not okay. Haven't you heard? I'm a freak, a cat-boy. My life is in danger, people are after me. There was an attempt on my life just a week ago. Other than that, I am okay, I guess…"

He thought of how freeing and liberating being able to say those words would feel. He was tired of lying, of pretending to be someone he wasn't, of keeping secrets especially from her. He longed to be accepted and loved for who he was, whatever that implied.

But instead he heard himself say, "Yes, I'm okay, was just grounded, that's all. My mom took my phone away."

"How come you weren't in school either?"

"I wasn't up for it, had the flu. I think I'm better now though."

"Hey, you back! Great to see you, bro. How you been?" Jake bumped him on his shoulder. "Ready?"

"Yeah, as ready as I'm going to be. Great to see you too."

"The bell's about to ring, have to get to class. See you at lunch?" He bent down and kissed Krissy on the lips. "Miss you so much! We'll catch up later, okay?"

"K, miss you too."

Jake and Houdini were walking to first period now. They had the same class together. Houdini didn't know how to begin the conversation.

"So, have you heard anything else?"

"Nope, nothing. Everything has been pretty quiet this last week. Did you tell your mom about what went down on New Year's Eve?"

"Nah, don't want to worry her more than she is right now. You tell your dad?" asked Houdini.

"No, haven't seen him, but still I wouldn't have told him. He is still MIA."

"Talking about what happened, I forgot to thank you for saving my life."

"Nah, it wasn't like that. Really! We are good."

"I was brave—"

"Hey, we are here! Let's go in. You don't want to be late your first day back, do you?"

"I really mean it…"

"I know… let's go."

Chapter 23

It was now spring. The snow had melted from the ground, and the tree showed different hues of green—from the very light green of fresh growth to the dark green of the pine trees and evergreens. The days were bright and sunny. The air smelled fresh and crisp. Houdini felt optimistic about the future. So far there had been no other news reports about the warehouse investigation and no other sighting of his persecutors. Maybe it was all behind him now, he thought, hopeful.

His days were spent like any other teenage boy does between school, spending time with Krissy, and now that spring was finally here, he had joined a soccer team. His coach was really impressed with his agility and speed, and they were already talking about future scholarship.

He loved soccer. Something about chasing a ball around just came natural to him. He had grown a couple of inches in the last months, and he felt stronger. Playing soccer gave him the chance to use his feline skills without calling attention to himself. Changing shapes was second nature to him now; he knew how to control it and when to make happen.

He had a little more freedom now that Jake was driving. His dad had surprised him for his sixteenth birthday with a brand-new black Mustang convertible right after he got his driving license. He drove Kevin and Houdini to school every day. No more school buses for them.

Houdini's cell phone rang on the way to his last period, well, more like vibrated, but he answered either way.

"Hey, bro! You are not going to believe what just happened."

"Jake? I'm seeing you right after class. What's so important that just can't wait?"

"Listen to this. I was standing by my locker just now when Keith just came up to me to invite us to a house party he is having at his house this Saturday."

"Dude, that's crazy. Are you sure?"

"Yeah. He said something about changing and feeling guilty about the way he treated us in the past, I don't know."

"What did you tell him?"

"Nothing. I took the flyer and walked away. It's all weird."

"What? Do you think he meant it?"

"I don't know, and to be honest, I don't really care. People like him don't change. A bully will always be a bully."

"People change sometimes. Maybe we should give him a second chance," said Houdini. "I don't know. We'll talk about it later, I guess. Did it look like it will be a happening party?"

"Maybe. There are flyers all over the school."

*****

Saturday, at around nine pm, they were driving on the way to Keith's house, still not sure if it was a good idea but willing to put the past behind them. Keith had offered an olive branch, and they wanted to believe it was true.

The neighborhood wasn't in one of the best areas in town, and they were having seconds thoughts about the whole thing.

"We have to show up now. We already said we would. If we don't show up now, he is going to take it personal," said Houdini.

"You sure, bro? I have a bad feeling about this."

"What can happen? We'll have a good time. We don't even have to socialize with him if we don't want to. There'll be plenty of people there."

As they approached the house, the loud music made their car tremble. There were people all over the front yard; they had a very hard time finding a place to park the car. They eventually found an empty spot about a block away.

As they walked into the house, they recognized some of the people from school, no one they were friends with, mostly Keith's friends and some of the populars. The air was thick with smoke. Vapor, they supposed. There didn't seem to be any adult supervision. Mrs. Wellington would have never consented to them going if it wasn't because he lied and said he was going to spend the night at Jake's.

Some of the girls were grinding against guys. Some seemed to be inebriated. There were empty beer cans over pretty much every surface in the room.

"Hey, I'm so glad you guys could make it," said Keith, walking out of the basement toward them, holding a beer. "Make yourself at home." It was really hard to hear him over the music. "Do you guys want something to drink?"

"What?"

Louder this time, "Do you want something to drink?"

"No. Not yet, maybe later."

They didn't drink alcohol, but they were trying to make themselves look cool.

"Suit yourself. Enjoy," he said, walking away and disappearing into the basement.

A chill went down Houdini's back. Something wasn't right.

He regretted coming to the party the minute they stepped in the house, but now it was kind of too late. He should've have listened to Jake.

They tried to make themselves comfortable, but they felt very uneasy about the whole situation. The people, what was going on there—everything felt wrong. Around 11:00 p.m. they decided to call it quits and head home. They hadn't seen Keith all night. As they were walking out the door, they noticed two black figures at either side of the gate. They looked like bouncers or bodyguards. But why would Keith need either one of those? His blood froze, and his heart stopped for a moment as he realized what was going on. They looked at each other, understanding without words. This was a setup. They were trapped. There was no way out. Houdini's heart was pounding so hard in his ears he could hardly think straight. Fear paralyzed him.

They both began to walk backward toward the house without taking their eyes away from the two men. Maybe if they walked slowly enough, they wouldn't be seen by them.

Houdini's legs were trembling as he walked back. His whole body was tense, his mind in a panic, when he felt two hands gripping him from the back. On instinct he swirled and got himself free. As he looked back, he saw Keith standing at the door with a grin on his face as two other men reached to grab him. Everything was happening too fast to think. It was surreal. He tried to run and tripped, falling face-down on the grass as he saw the other two men running toward him. He had never been so afraid in his life. He looked up and saw Jake disappearing over the fence. It wasn't Jake they were after. They let him go.

"Get to the car!" Jake yelled back at Houdini. "I'm going to get help. I'm calling the police."

The four men avalanche themselves over Houdini. The weight of them was too much. He could hardly breathe. Blood was rushing to his head. He felt dizzy, and then he squirmed free from under the man, running as fast as a cat can run in the direction of their parked car.

Jake was driving in the opposite direction when he spotted the black cat coming his way. He quickly opened the door, allowing it to jump right in.

He pressed the accelerator with all his might. The car tires screeched on the pavement. Through the rearview mirror, Jake saw two men jump in a car to follow them.

"Go go go!" said Houdini from the passenger side. "They are gaining way."

"I'm going as fast as I can. I don't know my way around here."

"Keep going, keep going!" As he said those words, the felt his body go forward against the dashboard and the steering wheel and back again.

"Did they just ram the car?" asked Jake in disbelief.

"Go faster!" Another ram on the back of the car made the car swerve.

"Floor it!" Houdini yelled. "We have to lose them."

He was trying to accelerate when the other car appeared right next to them. The car moved to the left and then slammed into the side of the car, making Jake lose control. The car was zigzagging on the road.

"I can't see! There's a curve. I'm going too fast," Jake said in a panic.

Another ram on the back side of the car made him lose control of the steering wheel. The car turned on its side with a loud bang! They felt themselves being thrown from one side of the car to the other side like weightless paper. The car was sliding on the pavement, glass breaking, metal scraping the asphalt, sparks flashing in the night. And blackness.

Chapter 24

Houdini opened his eyes and for a minute was disoriented. He was lying on a bed. He tried to move his arm and felt something holding it back. He freaked; he wanted to scream. He looked around in a panic. Then he saw a woman dressed in scrubs walking in the room.

"He is awake!" he heard her scream at someone.

She came running to his bedside, hovering over him.

"Where am I?" he asked, his voice raspy.

"You are at the hospital. You were in a car accident. You have been out for a couple of days. How are you feeling?"

Before he could answer, he looked around, trying to make sense of what he was hearing. The room seemed to be empty except for his hospital bed. The fluorescent lights above made him squint. His mouth felt dry. There was a curtain dividing the room for privacy, but there did not seem to be anyone on the bed next to his.

There was an IV on his right hand. He saw the liquid dripping from the IV bag into the tube and into his vein. On the other side of the bed was a heart monitor; the number on the machine flashed 80, with a beeping sound, *Beep, beep, beep.* He tried moving his legs. His legs moved. He tried to move his toes; they moved too. He felt relieved.

"I'm okay, I guess. What happened?"

"I don't know all the details. They brought you over in an ambulance last Saturday night. You were unconscious. We've been keeping an eye over you. The doctor will be in later today. You can ask all the questions then. I'm glad you are doing better. For a minute there we thought we lost you." She grabbed his arm and wrapped a black band around it closed it with Velcro and pumped air into it to check his blood pressure, 110/70, a little low but good.

"Wait. Have someone been here to see me?"

"Yes, there have been a few people. Your mom just went home. She's been here for days. She needed a break. I will phone her and let her know you're up," she said while she held a thermometer in front of his face. "Under your tongue," she said. She waited a few minutes, looked at it, and said, "Ninety-eight."

"Let me check your pupils," she said, pointing a light into his eyes. Houdini was blinded for a minute. "Follow the light," she said as she pointed the light from right to left and then up and down.

"Good." She got up to go. "Ah, before I forget, the police will be here later now that you're up. They want to ask you some questions. And don't mind the men outside the door. They are just guarding your room." She touched his forehead and walked away.

The police? People guarding my room? What?

His head hurt. He used his free hand to rub his temple. He tried hard to remember.

The last he recalled, they were at Keith's party, his heart racing, the men, the chase… He was breathing heavy now. *And Jake! Oh no, is he okay?* Reality hit him like a ton of bricks.

Before he even had time to take it all in, there were two police officers entering his room. One was holding a pad and pen.

"Good day, son, we need to ask you a couple of questions about the accident. I hope you don't mind. We are investigating the case. Are you up for it?"

"I… I…"

"It won't take long. I promise."

The interview was over in about twenty minutes. Houdini told them all he remembered from that night. He learned that someone had called the authority. The police got there soon after the accident. There were witnesses to the chase, and the two men were apprehended after they tried fleeing the accident site on foot. There was a pending investigation into the case, and they could not say more.

"What happened to my friend? The one driving? Is he okay?"

"We are not in liberty to comment on the matter. You are going to have to ask someone else about that. Thank you for your time, and here's our card. If you remember anything else, don't hesitate to give us a call." And with that they walked out of the room.

He was left more confused than before. Did they know who the men were? Did they know all this was related to the ongoing investigation of the warehouse? Did they know who he was?

The room was spinning. His head felt heavy, and he blacked out.

He woke up again a day later. Mrs. Wellington was at his bedside. He felt weak, his eyelids felt heavy, and his mouth was as dry as cotton. But he had never been happier to see anyone before.

Mrs. Wellington hugged him and kissed his forehead and caressed his hair. "Oh my god, you are back. How are you feeling?"

He thought about it. He did not feel too good, but he heard himself say, "I'm okay, Mom. How is Jake?"

Mrs. Wellington's eyes filled with tears as she handed Houdini the newspaper she was keeping in her purse.

"What's this?"

"Just read it, honey," she said, looking down, avoiding Houdini's stare.

Adjusting to the light to see, Houdini grabbed the paper. There in the front page was a picture of the accident site. Houdini couldn't believe what he was seeing. The Mustang was totaled on its side and crashed into a telephone pole. His heart skipped a beat. He looked to Mrs. Wellington, but she looked away. He continued to the captions. It read, "Car chase ends in fatal accident." The word *fatal* jumped out of the page. His brain didn't register, or maybe it did. It was his heart that could not take it. His throat was tightening, and his eyes were burning. He could not catch a breath. *No, no, this has to be a mistake. It could not be possible… Jake isn't dead.*

He looked as his mom. "Mom, please tell me it's not true. Is it?" he pleaded as he fell back into bed, sobbing. He never knew pain like this before; it hurt too much. His heart was broken in a million pieces, never to be whole again.

Everything after that was a daze. He would not eat. He cried so much that he had no tears left to cry. He had to be put on antidepressants. By the time he left the hospital a week later, he had lost almost ten pounds.

The day of Jake's wake was the worst day of his life so far. Even all the abuse he had endured in the past paled in comparison to the pain he felt.

The funeral parlor was full. Almost the whole school attended. There was no urn, no casket, just pictures of Jake. And flowers, lots of flowers. It all felt so unreal.

People took turns talking about Jake and the memories they had of him. When it was his turn to talk, his throat got so tight he could not speak a word, so he passed.

Jake's dad was the last one to go up to the front to honor Jake's memories.

He walked over to one of the tables and picked one of Jake's pictures, the one where they were together on a fishing trip. Jake was smiling proudly, holding a fish. He must've been around ten years old. His father's arms were around his shoulder. The whole room was silent. You could hear a fly. As he was talking about his memories of that day, he got very emotional. Jake's dad sat down crying on one of the steps, his hand covering his nose and mouth as he cried over the picture.

And then… Houdini finally saw the face that was part of every nightmare he ever had. The masked face, the one he was never able to identify, was right there in front of him, in front of everyone, crying over his dead son.

In a flash, everything came back to Houdini's mind. He was the scientist—the doctor that had experimented on him, maybe even created him. Now it all made sense—the medical books Jake took from his dad where they found the symbol of his collar, his dad always gone whenever something bad happened to them. Also, he was a local. It would've been very easy for him to take the cat's cage to the Humane Society. And Jake? Houdini's mind was going through a million thoughts a minute now. He felt faint. Jake was odd… autistic. *Wait a minute,* he thought to himself. *Could it be? Could have Jake been the other stolen embryo?*

Jake's dad was the scientist, he had no doubt. He was the one behind all this. Houdini's whole body was trembling with anger and hate. He knew he hated him. He hated him with every fiber of his being. He was going to get his revenge. But how? What was he going to do about it?

That, he had to think about very hard and carefully before acting. He had to keep it a secret until the right time and place. Not now, not here. This was about Jake.

He held his mother's hand and Kevin's just to feel connected and safe. He would tell them soon enough, he thought to himself.

Chapter 25

The day after Jake's wake, Houdini woke up to madness all around him. Apparently, someone had taken a cell phone video of what had occurred outside Keith's house the night of the party and had sold it to the news.

The house phone was ringing off the hook. There were all kinds of TV station and radio station vans parked outside the house, and every newspaper reporter in the world was there, it seemed like.

The video, which had gone viral by now, showed Houdini changing from boy to cat right in front of the camera for everyone to see.

Houdini's mom answered yet another call from a TV show asking for Houdini to appear in the show—everyone from CBN to Fox News to *Good Morning America*. Everyone wanted to be the first one to present the boy-cat or cat-boy to the world.

As Mrs. Wellington tried to keep the reporter at bay, Kevin helped Houdini get a book bag and duffel bag ready with clean clothes, water, and food.

"Where will you go, bro?"

"I don't know yet. But I have to leave as soon as possible. You know I'm not safe here anymore."

"Here, take my cellphone. I'm sure they'll track yours. Don't call me. I will call you when it's safe to do so."

Houdini hugged his family tight. Anna was holding on to him in tears. Mrs. Wellington stuck some money in his pocket. "Be safe," she said, kissing him on the cheek, and with that, he escaped through the back door, into the woods.

Two weeks had passed since the day Houdini had to escape his own house. That day was a tough day for him not knowing what to do and being afraid to be found out. He walked aimlessly through the woods. He had to maintain his human form in order to carry the provisions, which made him more noticeable too. He thought he was being followed more than once. But it turned out to be his imagination. It was getting late and he was exhausted from walking, when he remembered the old abandoned house where he took refuge when he ran away as a cat.

It was nighttime by the time he made it there. The house was still abandoned.

Just as he remembered it so, he took refuge there. He made sure to hide from sight during the day, and at nighttime he would roam the back streets as a cat. He had to keep out of sight so he had no access to a television and didn't really know what was going on.

He tried not to use Kevin's cell phone because he was trying to save the battery life just in case Kevin would try to call him. With all the commotion on the day he left, he had forgotten to take the cell phone charger.

With all the free time he had on his hands, he couldn't stop thinking about Jake and all that had happened. He felt responsible for Jake's death. If only he had listened to him and not gone to the party, he would still be alive. His heart broke at the thought of never seeing him again. Jake was his only friend. He had befriended Houdini and accepted him from day one. He knew who Houdini was but liked him just the same. He had even jumped in front of a moving car to save his life. And he couldn't save his.

The more he thought about the possibility of Jake being the second stolen embryo, the more it made sense to him. That day when Jake jumped in front of the car to save his life, the car had turned to the side to avoid hitting him. Every time they were being persecuted, Jake was never the target even when sometimes he was right in front of their persecutors. He was not taken or run after. It was all too clear to him now; they had never been after Jake.

And if that was the case and Jake was the second embryo, then he felt he had more of a reason to hate Jake's dad.

He had picked one embryos to love care for and raise as a son, while he had used the other one (him) to torture and experiment with.

He worried about Krissy too. By now she knew the truth about who he was. It was all over the news, he was sure of that. Would she still love him? Or would she think him a freak? Not being able to communicate with anyone was killing him. But he had to stay hidden—his life depended on it.

He was startled by the cell phone ringing. He answered on the first ring. It was Kevin on the other line.

"Where are you? Is it safe to talk?"

"Yes, it's all good. How about you? Are you okay?"

"I am."

"Had the publicity died down?" asked Houdini.

"Not really. Well, maybe a little. But we need to talk. Where are you?"

"I'll text you the address. Can't be on the phone long. My phone battery—well, *your* phone is dying. Make sure you come at nighttime. Don't let anybody see you."

"Will do. Stay safe." And with that Kevin hung up.

Houdini's provisions were running low. He decided to make a run to the local supermarket and used the money that Mrs. Wellington had given him to buy food and water. He didn't know how long it would be before he was able to go home again, maybe never, by the looks of it. He grabbed the money from his book bag and put it inside his shoe. He raised the top of his black hoodie to conceal his face and looked both ways as he left the barn to make sure no one was watching. He left the house on foot, going through the back streets to a convenience store he had seen on the way to the abandoned house. There weren't many people at the store at that time, and the few that were there did not pay attention to him. After getting the supplies he came to get, he approached the checkout line, trying to act as normal as possible, making sure not to bring any attention to himself. As he was paying for the groceries, he looked at the magazine racks right next to the register, looking down to conceal his face. He could not believe his eyes. His face was in every magazine, every newspaper and tabloid. He grabbed one of them and put it in his cart, trying not make eye contact with the clerk. He paid for everything and left the store in a hurry the same way he had come, thankful that no one had recognized him and making sure that no one was following him.

When he got to the house, he opened the magazine to the many pages and articles about him. There was an article about the possibility of him being an alien. There were scientists who speculated that he was part of the evolution of an unknown species. There were some who believed he was a mutant or a freak, and others that believed he was some kind of superhero. There were people wearing his shirt, his infamous black hoodie with the upside-down triangle. And most kids from school were claiming to be friends with him even though he did not know or recognize any of them. It was all a big circus, he thought to himself. He tucked the magazine back in his bag and waited for Kevin to show up that night.

Kevin got the text with the address where Houdini was staying. He would wait for sundown before he would try to find Houdini. He felt that his every move was being watched, and he didn't want to jeopardize Houdini's safety or give up his location. Krissy would join him. They had kept in contact through this whole ordeal. She knew who Houdini was by now. Kevin had explained everything to her—how they had adopted the cat from the Humane Society, how it became a kid over time. She knew the entire story except what they knew about the cloning and stolen embryos. He didn't want to tell her at first, but she wouldn't give up. She would show up at the house almost every day. She followed him at school constantly, asking question about Houdini, until he felt he had no choice but to tell her, but only right after he sworn her to secrecy. Now she knew almost everything about Houdini's story, but she didn't care. It didn't change the way she felt about him. She loved him more than ever now that she knew he was in danger, and she was willing to do anything to be with him.

The house had been closely watched for days. They were constantly under surveillance from the countless news reporters parked outside the house. The publicity about the cat video was still insane.

They waited until after 12:00 a.m. to leave the house. Krissy had told her parents that she was sleeping a Stacey's tonight.

They left through the back door, trying very hard not to be seem. They had to go by foot. The ATVs would be way too loud at this time of night, and they did not want to be found out or followed. They went the way Houdini had instructed them through the woods, constantly looking over their shoulders.

After what seemed to be hours of walking, they finally made it to Houdini's location.

The abandoned house was pitch-black when they got to it. Luckily, there didn't seem to be anyone awake at that time, and they were able to get in the house without being seen. Houdini was waiting for him inside. He was expecting to see Kevin alone. He cried tears of joy when he saw Krissy appearing at the door.

They hugged for a while, not being able to let go of each other.

When they finally sat down to talk, Kevin explained to Houdini what had happened since he had left the house.

After the two men were apprehended, under pressure from the authorities and the FBI, they had confessed to being part of the warehouse staff, the animal abuse, etc.; and after being threatened to be charged with Jake's death and being sent to jail for the rest of their lives, they gave away all the information they had on Jake's dad. The police had their man now. But there was only one problem. They had no evidence against him that could be proven in a court of law without making the whole case public and bringing everything to the light, and that was something they were not willing to do. They would have to confess about the human cloning, about the knowledge of the missing embryos, about the poor investigation into the case at the time, etc. The repercussions were going to be bigger than they were willing to face.

So as a result of all this, they were offering Houdini a deal. They needed Houdini to testify against Jake's dad in a closed-court case in order to properly persecute him. They needed Houdini's testimony about what he knew and the abuse he had endured from them. They needed to get evidence from Houdini's DNA. They would have to run tests on Houdini, test his blood and DNA, in order to have proof of wrongdoing. And in exchange for this, they would clear Houdini's name. He and his family would be granted immunity and would go into the witness protection program. He would be granted a new identity, or an identity since he never had one. He would be given a birth certificate and a social security card. He would be given the right to start a new life as a normal person.

Houdini could not believe what he was hearing. It was all too good to be true.

"So would you take the deal?" asked Kevin.

"I don't know. How do I know they are telling the truth and not trying to track me down for God knows what?"

Krissy hugged him tight. "This would be the only chance that we would be able to be together. To have a normal life," she murmured. "You have to take, Houdini. This is our only chance."

"Yes, Houdini, Krissy is right. This is your only chance to be normal, the only way that you would not have to give your family up, Mom, Anna, and me. If you don't take this deal, you would have to be in the run forever. You would have to give up your life."

He knew what they were saying was true. This was his only chance at a normal life, but the fear was still keeping him hostage.

Chapter 26

On the day of the trial, Houdini was escorted by security into the courtroom. The case was not made public.

In front of a judge, he had finally the chance to confront his abuser face-to-face, to confront his fears, to accuse him in front of everyone, and to tell him how he felt about him and what he had done to him. All the information that had been collected from Houdini's blood test and DNA were used as evidence against him.

Throughout the whole trial, Jake's dad refused to utter a word. Even after being confronted by Houdini himself, he continued to stare into space without showing any emotion.

The trial lasted a week. After hearing the testimony of the scientist and doctors about Houdini's condition, he was sentenced to life in prison without the possibility of parole. He remained emotionless as he was escorted in handcuffs out of the courtroom.

Houdini was granted immunity. He was not to be experimented on or bothered in any way. And all the publicity about the cat-boy was explained away in the news.

The YouTube video had shown a boy that had turned into a cat. But the face of the boy was not shown in the video. The image was too dark for the face to be recognizable. The only reason they had gone after Houdini was because of Keith's accusation. But the media was able to turn it around by saying that in fact it had been Jake, not Houdini, who had turned into a cat and that his body had been cremated before the video went viral, so there was no evidence that proved him being a cat—if that was even possible. They claimed the video was a hoax created for publicity and shock factor. And the interest on the video finally died out. It was only Keith's word against Houdini's. The rest of the people at the party were too intoxicated to remember what had actually happened or to be credible witnesses. The only one who continued to claim that it was Houdini who had turned into a cat was Keith. But who would believe Keith?

*****

Houdini woke up early in the morning. It was the first day back on his own bed. He lingered in bed, thinking about everything that had transpired in last couple of months. He still could not believe that Jake was gone. He thought about him every day, and his heart broke every time. Eventually, it would get better, he knew that. Time heals all wounds. But he knew he would never forget him for as long as he lived, as long as that might be. He breathed the fresh air coming through the open window. This was his first day here. From his room he heard Anna running after the cat down the stairs. "Hey, kitty-kitty, come back."

Kevin opened the door of Houdini's room and stuck his head in.

"Hey, are you up? Breakfast is ready. Hurry up. We don't want to be late."

Yeah, he thought to himself, he was the luckiest person alive. He had a family to belong to and a future and a life. He didn't have to hide who he was anymore or be constantly looking over his shoulder.

Today in a new city and a new high school, he was starting a new life as Adam Jake, and nobody knew who he was except Krissy.

And of course Keith, but he wasn't going to worry about that now, not today.

Today was the first day of the rest of his life.

About the Author

Mayra Araujo is a Cuban American fiction writer. She left Cuba with her parents during her teen years and lived in Miami, Florida, for many years, where she learned the language and acquired a passion for reading and writing. Creativity has always been a part of her being. She enjoys painting and interior decorating, as well as creating wonderful fictional characters everyone is sure to love. God and family are at the center of all she does, and she credits them with all blessing and success that come her way. Today she lives in Woodstock, Georgia, with her husband of twenty-three years and her two young adult children. She is a member of the Writing Tribe; Women Writers, Women's Books; and the Georgia Writer Association.

CPSIA information can be obtained
at www.ICGtesting.com
Printed in the USA
LVHW040915280820
664155LV00004B/515